The Debt
Collector

a novel by

Jon Mills

Direct Response Publishing

ISBN-13: 978-1516811854
ISBN-10: 1516811852

Also By Jon Mills

Dedication

To those who see gold
beneath dross even
when others
don't.

1

RIKERS PRISON WAS HELL *on an island.* Jack paced back and forth in his cell for hours that morning. After four years, he felt more uncomfortable this day than he had when he first arrived.

The last year in and out of solitary confinement for fighting had only made it worse. Twenty-three hours holed up in a six by eight cell, surrounded by nothing more than cinder blocks, a bunk, a sink and a toilet; it changed a man. It was known to break even the toughest, to push anyone to their mental limits and beyond. The men referred to it as "the box," and even that didn't quite describe the claustrophobic feeling you felt. The thought of never getting out haunted him daily.

Today was no different. There was always doubt eating away at the back of his mind. He'd seen men's wills get thrown to the curb minutes before they saw the outside. Now, however, as the familiar sound of steel toe boots striking against the steely catwalk approached his door, it brought a welcome relief. The twist of the key in the lock and the clanging of the metal flap had become a part of his daily routine.

This morning, though, was different. It would be the last time he would hear it. Between the small mesh window he saw two new prison guards. The faces changed frequently; not because of shift rotation, but because few lasted beyond a couple of months in this place. He turned his back, stuck his hands through the hole behind him, and felt the click of metal around his wrists. He winced, feeling the metal teeth pinch his skin.

"Inmate, take two steps forward."

Led by the guards, Jack shuffled along the upper tier, greeted by the usual sounds of rage. Men and teens screamed obscenities, banging on the metal doors while others smeared their own feces through the mesh. It never let up, day or night. It was pure chaos. You just learned to block out the constant hollering.

They escorted him through a series of security doors, each one bringing home the reality that it was finally over. He was ushered into a small room where he could collect his belongings. He changed out of the prison garments and slipped back into his stonewashed jeans, black t-shirt, and leather jacket. While it felt good to have his belongings back, something was missing: sixteen bucks and twenty-five cents, to be precise. That's exactly what he'd had on him when he'd entered. Conveniently enough, that was nowhere to be found now. He scoffed, knowing it had probably been used to buy the guards a case of beer.

Outside he squinted, his eyes adjusting to the brightness of the warm summer morning. He breathed in the deep salty air. Led up to the gates, he waited behind a thick yellow line as the aging steel cracked open. Cupping a hand over his eyes, the blinding orange rays of the sun blocked his view. It took him but a second to recognize the silhouette leaning up against a souped up Pinto: Freddy Carlone. He was one of Roy Gafino's piss ants. They were cut from the same cloth and equally responsible for his incarceration.

"Jack."

A cigarette hung out the corner of the man's mouth. He spread his arms wide open. Ignoring him, Jack took a hard right, strolling past him. Freddy fell in step.

"No hug for an old buddy?"

Jack remained silent, forging forward.

"Jack?"

He heard the crunch of gravel as the Pinto crawled behind them.

"It's a long walk back. Come on, let me give you a ride."

He kept walking.

"Jack, c'mon, it'll be like old times. I'll buy you a drink. You can't still be bitter after a few years?"

Jack stopped abruptly, spun around, and grabbed him by the scruff of the neck. The Pinto came to a halt and Louis bolted out of the driver's side. Freddy waved him off.

"Four years, thirteen days, seven hours, and thirty four minutes."

There was a tense pause.

Freddy threw his hands up. "Okay, okay."

Jack slowly released his grip on him.

"Look, Roy asked me to pick you up. He wants to see you."

"I have nothing to say."

"Yeah, well, you know how it works."

Jack studied his face for a minute, cast a glance off in the direction he had been heading, and then reluctantly walked over to the car and got in. Inside, Louis leaned over, banging a carton of Camels in his hand.

"Cigarette?"

***

Dana Grant's morning hadn't gone exactly as planned. Sitting in an uncomfortable chair outside the principal's office, she gazed down at her crumpled to-do list. Nowhere on it had she listed a visit to Rockland Cove

High School. Until ten o'clock that morning, actually, she had been under the impression that her fourteen-year-old son was sitting comfortably at a desk in one of his classes. Now everything had to take a backseat. That included phone calls to get quotes for repairs on the motel, a long overdue return call to the deputy sheriff, and a chat with the animal hospital to arrange pick up of the ashes of their recently cremated dog.

She glanced at her reflection in the glass cabinet that contained numerous regional awards, smoothing a few loose strands of black hair back into place. That was another thing—she sorely needed to get her hair done. The thought lasted only seconds before moving to the reason she had been called in. Her needs came second to her son's. She didn't resent that fact, since it had been a rough year for them both. In many ways, it was to be expected.

"Dana."

Susan Walsh, the principal of the school, came out of her office. The woman had known her since childhood. She was a sweet person, but she did have a tendency to highlight Dana's flaws any chance she got. At least, that was the impression Dana got. They both had a keen interest in teaching, but Susan was the only one who had moved from dreaming to achievement. It was no fault of Dana's; getting pregnant at eighteen and having no parents around to help had seriously slammed the brakes on her own pursuit. In many ways, after seeing how Susan had turned out, she was glad.

The need to keep up appearances and be politically correct with every parent—it didn't exactly appeal to her. She was a woman who tended to speak her mind. She considered herself a free spirit. She valued all the things that Susan appeared to have lost when making the transition from teen to adult.

Growing up is what they called it; becoming mature and responsible. It was a badge she'd worn with honor, and in many ways she owned it, yet simmering under the surface was a free spirit longing to be released. She wanted to experience a life without restrictions, responsibilities— not to mention morning meetings with beady-eyed principals who looked down on her.

Susan swept her hand toward her office, as if ushering in a child who had zero directional skills. Dana pursed her lips and stepped inside.

"Please, take a seat."

Dana sat squarely across from Susan, a mahogany desk between them. Various photo frames of Susan's family were scattered across the room's shelves and tables, and two children who reminded Dana of robots smiled with pearly white teeth back at her. As Susan observed her, she couldn't help but feel as if her life was under inspection.

An engraved nameplate sat in front of her—a simple reminder of Susan's title in life, or a reminder of who she was? Either way, it niggled Dana. She had an urge to flip it around the other way, but undoubtedly Susan's name was on the other side too so she could fluff her ego throughout the day like a vain person checking a mirror every chance they got.

"How are you, Dana?" Susan asked, in her most condescending voice.

"Fine."

Susan scanned her face as if trying to spot a crack in what she had come to expect every mother wore: a mask. Satisfied or just eager to get down to business, she flipped her computer screen around.

"This is a list of the days your son has attended school. Do you see anything wrong with this?"

Other than your reflection in the screen? Dana thought.

"Well, this can't be right. I've dropped him off every day here."

Susan twisted the screen back around, taking a deep breath. Dana knew she was readying the speech she had prepared to give her whole life. The one that brought Dana up to speed on how kids really acted, and how responsible parents, ones not running a run-down motel, should be. Susan opened her mouth, then closed it.

"What am I missing here, Susan?"

"It's not what you're missing. It's what your son is. He has been absent for close to thirty days over the past year."

Dana didn't hesitate in responding to what she could tell was more of an accusation against her than against her son. "Well, why have you not informed me of this sooner?"

Susan reached into the drawer in front of her and retrieved a folded piece of paper. She slid it to Dana, raising her eyebrows in the process.

"It appears your son has been forging your signature."

Dana's brow knit together as she unfolded the paper. Sure enough, there was her signature, as clear as day. However, it wasn't hers. It wasn't bad, actually, but there was a slight difference in the letter G.

"I, of course, recognized the forgery the moment I saw it."

Yes, I'm sure you did. Dana rolled her eyes.

"You see, he's not the first teen that has attempted to pull the wool over our eyes, but thankfully our small town keeps a close eye on those who happen to be lingering outside Tina's restaurant, the library, or the marina during school hours. From there, I pulled one of your older letters."

"You keep them?"

"Certainly. How else do you expect us to catch them?"

Quite the Agatha Christie, aren't we? Dana thought.

"Well, be assured I will be having words with him. I appreciate you letting me know."

"Is there anything at home that might be of concern?"

"At home? If anything, this is more likely related to school."

"Right." She nodded slowly, as if unable to comprehend that any student would find Rockland High School anything less than a paradise. "Well, I was referring to the situation with his father."

"That is our business."

"But when it affects his schoolwork, it becomes ours."

Dana stood. "I appreciate your concern, and this will be taken care of."

"Please, Dana. If there is anything we can do to help—for now we'll let this all slide."

Susan stood, extending her hand. Dana glanced at it, hesitating before shaking it and leaving with what remained of her dignity.

2

ROY GAFINO headed up one of five crime families that operated out of the New Jersey area. He ran a seedy but notorious boxing gym in Bergen County called The Pig's Ear. This was where Jack had first met him, back when he was fourteen. The gym had become an escape from the constant beatings he received at home. His father never thought twice about laying into him. He typically didn't need a reason, but when there was one—those were the memorable nights. Fists, leather belts, you name it. It didn't matter to him; whatever was within reach was game.

His stepmother wasn't any better. If she thought he took too long to complete a chore, she wouldn't hesitate to swat him. It was never with her hand; she always used a broomstick or something similar. Hands were for loving, she would say. She'd once broken a broom handle over his back, an incident they'd found hard to cover up when he wasn't in school for several weeks. Yeah, when she was conscious, she was just as much a lunatic as her husband.

Maybe that's why he had been drawn to Gafino. There was sense of family in the gym. A brotherhood. While he knew the place had an unsavory reputation, he also knew that if you were in with them, no one would touch you. They looked out for each other; at least, that's how it appeared. In the early days, Gafino had spotted Jack's natural talent for boxing and took him under his wing. It wasn't long before he was running errands for him, transporting packages to locations throughout New Jersey. Jack always had a good sense of what he was delivering, but he never questioned it. In their line of business, you didn't ask questions. Questions led to complications and mistakes. Mistakes got you killed. That became even clearer at the age of eighteen, when Jack committed his first hit.

As they drove across the bridge between Rikers and the borough of Queens, Jack gazed out at the East River; his mind was lost in memories of those early days.

"You want to make more money, Jack?" Gafino asked.

"Yeah. Sure."

"If I told you to pull the trigger, could you do it?"

He shrugged. "I guess."

"You guess, or you could without any question?"

"Yeah, I could."

Those three words took him down a road that could have only led to one of two destinations: prison or a bullet in the back of the head. That day had replayed in his mind countless times over the past ten years. The whispers of old memories always found their way to the surface, like ugly faces that tormented his mind. It's said that there is loyalty among thieves, but nothing could be further from the truth. In the twenty years he'd worked for Gafino, he'd seen friends turn on friends over a simple insult. Then you had those who were jealous and wanted to make a name for themselves by climbing the ladder. Others—well, they became snitches.

Jack knew the dangers of being associated with the Gafinos, and yet they were all he'd known for as long as he could remember. They had taken the place of his own family; they were the ones who had put clothes on his back, gave him a job, and looked out for him. Even after he had moved out of his parents' place, they gave him a place to sleep. Doing time just came with the territory. Hell, it was rare to find anyone who hadn't done time for one thing or another. Murder, assault, drug dealing, arson—you name it, there was nothing that was beyond their means. Most knew that; once out of prison they would go right back to doing what they had without batting an eye. It was all they knew.

For Jack, however, it was different this time. A short

stint in a cell was one thing, but being locked up for more than four years was another. Surrounded by cement and bars had given him time to think about his life. He wasn't getting any younger, and he was in a business that ran on fear, intimidation, and mistrust. He knew it would only be a matter of time before he'd find himself wrapped in bags, a bullet in his skull, or sinking to the bottom of the Hudson River with his feet in cement. He was surprised he'd lasted this long.

Jack hadn't spoken to any of them since being locked up, and the thought of renewing his friendship with them again wasn't in the cards. Thinking about going his separate way had once been out of the question, but now it was the only thing he'd been sure about in a long time. It wasn't as if they had visited him while he was inside. Wasn't that what family was supposed to do? He shook his head.

He hadn't seen it when he was young. His pride, naivety, and drive to make a name for himself had got the better of him. He'd risen through the ranks quickly. His methods were unorthodox, but they worked. There was never any room for error, no room for emotion. That's why they sent him in. When it was time to do a job, it was like flipping a switch. He had no rules, except one: no women or kids. But it was obvious that as long as you were of use to them they would walk over coals for you.

But at the slight chance you ceased to line their wallets or deliver, well…

Jack shot Freddy and Louis a quick glance before returning to watch the stream of traffic. He would keep his visit brief. He'd listen to what Roy had to say and then be on his way. Where he'd go from there didn't matter. He'd figure that out later.

**

Dana stared blankly at the middle-aged couple yelling at her. They hadn't been the first, and undoubtedly they wouldn't be the last. But as they reeled off every reason why their motel room was below human standards, she once again found herself recollecting better days. Months where rooms were full and she'd had to switch on the No Vacancy light. Of course, that had been long before the bypass was built, and… She zoned back in momentarily to swipe their card and refund their money.

Over the past year since the incident with Jason's father, Dana had somehow found a way to begin picking up the pieces. It hadn't been easy, and at times it felt as if she had crawled her way back to existence. If it hadn't been for Jason, she wasn't sure what she might have done. Summoning the energy to face each day felt more difficult than giving up. Even though her thinking was selfish, she understood how depression could drive a person to self-harm—or worse, take their life. While she hadn't reached that point, she had come dangerously close to the edge of the abyss. That was, of course, until she realized the implications of what she was thinking.

In the early days after the incident, she'd received phone calls daily for weeks. She'd wondered what they wanted to hear. Most of her friends meant well, and they tried to help her see the light at the end of the tunnel, so it wasn't as if she didn't have anyone to talk to about it. It was just that she had nothing to say. She felt numb, removed from the situation, dead inside as if somehow viewing herself from the outside. These weren't the kind of things you shared over coffee, in passing conversation, or even with a doctor—unless you wanted them to place you under observation. Instead, she told them what she assumed they wanted to hear. That while it was hard she was coping with meds her doctor had prescribed.

Yet in all honesty, she'd only taken the pills for a short while. They fogged up her mind, made her sleep the day away, and put her in a catatonic state. How could anyone return to living again under those conditions? She knew that if she let herself spiral down any further, continue taking the meds, there was no way of knowing if she would find her way back. So she quit taking them. The first couple of months, she hadn't stepped out of the house other than to drive Jason to school and collect a few groceries. Those days were the hardest. She felt the eyes of people on her as she pushed a cart around the local SuperMart; she heard the whispers and had a good idea of what people were saying.

Find the silver lining in every dark moment; her father would say that when she was little. She'd never forgotten it, or them, for that matter. God, how she missed her mother and father. Born and raised in Rockland Cove, they had been her strength throughout her life. A listening ear when things had fallen through with college, a pick-me-up when her heart was broken for the first time, and a lifesaver that saw her through an unexpected pregnancy.

She groaned inwardly. So much had changed over the years.

"You have a good day," she said, leaning on the office counter and watching the couple head off to the modern lodge in town.

If it hadn't been for the run of good years that they'd had, she wouldn't have been able to keep the place afloat. Goodwill, cooked meals from neighbors, and an ever-declining bank account balance only stretched so far. The truth was their financial difficulties had started long before that fateful night.

3

Pulling up around the back of The Pig's Ear, Jack noted how little had changed. It was a six-story brick building, with two fire escapes and underground tunnels that led away to other parts of the city. Like always, there were a few teens loitering around outside, and a couple of Gafino's men kept an eye out for police. At one time the building had been a respectable hotel, until Gafino muscled his way in and set up shop. Now it drew in a different kind of clientele.

The smell of sweat and testosterone hung in the air inside. The sounds of men sparring brought back a flood of fond memories and a pang inside his gut. Unlike the first day he walked in, this place was now the last place he wanted to be. Freddy grinned, jabbing his finger at individuals, shouting names as if he was doing a roll call. Hardened men scrutinized him. It was a mix of new and old faces; guys he'd had drinks with in the past, and those he'd never seen before.

Jack followed Freddy into the back, through a series of doors, and up a steel staircase. Every room he passed reminded him of the man he had once been. Was he different? Could four years really change who you were?

Entering Roy's office, they were greeted by the sight of a pale white ass and a brunette bent over his desk.

"How many fucking times do I have to tell you to knock?"

"Shit, sorry, boss."

Roy twisted around and gave them a look of disapproval before making eye contact with Jack. His face immediately lit up. A huge smile appeared.

He slapped the girl on the ass. She pulled her panties up and readjusted her dress before slipping past them, her face red with embarrassment. Roy fumbled with the belt buckle on his pants before approaching them.

"She looks a lot like Theresa, don't you think?"

Jack never replied. Theresa was the girl he'd been with before he had been locked up. Roy had taken a liking to her; some even said he was screwing her on the side. Jack didn't ask; he knew better.

"It's been a long time." He wrapped his arms around Jack.

"Yeah," Jack replied, his composure stoic.

"Freddy, pour the man a drink. This is cause for

celebration."

Freddy hustled over to an oak cabinet and retrieved a bottle of malt whiskey. After pouring a couple of glasses, he handed one to Jack.

"So, four years behind bars. It's been a long time since I last served. Do the inmates still make their own alcohol? What was it made of again?"

"Tomatoes—" Jack began.

"Sugar and yeast. That's right. Foul-tasting stuff, but I guess you can't be picky."

Jack felt the warm burn of the liquid as it slipped down his throat. For a moment he felt his muscles unwind. The reality that he was out was beginning to set in, but so was the thought of telling Roy that it was over.

"Come, take a seat."

"I'll stand."

Roy must have caught something in his reply. It was rare for anyone to do anything but what he said, even in what some might have taken as a simple suggestion.

"Take a seat." It was no longer a request.

Jack glanced at Freddy and Louis, who stood by the door. He breathed in deeply, placed his glass down, and took a seat. Roy slipped behind the desk and leaned back in the leather chair as if he was the king of New York. To those who knew him, he was. His rise to becoming a made man had not come without a fair amount of blood being spilled.

"Now that you're out, we can get back to business. I've got you set up with a new place. Tony took yours after you went in."

"That's the thing."

He was about to continue when there was a knock at the door.

"Come in."

"He's downstairs." A well-built man dressed in a suit shot Jack a look.

"Jack, Vincent. He's been filling your shoes while you were inside."

A look of animosity appeared on Vincent's face.

"As I was saying…" Jack continued, turning back to Gafino.

Roy stood up. "Hold that thought and follow me."

Reluctantly, Jack followed his entourage down the hallway and several flights of steps until he was in a dank basement.

He knew what this place was about.

Boxers didn't come down here. Few people ever saw the underground; that even included some of Roy's closest men. There were few reasons to be down here. Lights faintly lit the stone corridor. It smelled musty and damp. The tunnels had been built back in the 20s when prohibition was active. What had been a simple means of transferring alcohol and remaining undetected had become a new way to bring in drugs and cart out bodies. The granite stone made the area soundproof, and with the noise of the gym and streets above, few ever heard the final cries of those pleading for their lives.

Behind a locked wooden door, a man sat in a chair. He wore nothing more than a shirt and underpants. The room was empty, the floor stained red with large droplets of blood. He looked as if he had already taken a hard beating. His shirt was pulled back and there were several slashes across his chest. A bloodied rag carved deep into the skin around his mouth. His head hung low. The smell of piss lingered.

Gafino nodded to one of his men.

A man took a bucket of water and threw it over him. The man awoke, gasping and wild-eyed. Upon seeing Roy, he mumbled.

"Take the rag out."

The moment it was pulled, the pleading began. He was a blubbering mess. Between the tears and blood in his mouth, they could barely make out a word of what he said. Jack studied his swollen face, trying to place where he'd seen him before.

"Nicky, Nicky. How long have I known you?"

Little Nicky Civella. That was it. He'd been one of the kids in the neighborhood. Good kid. Crafty thief—

maybe a little too good. If there was anything that needed to be taken without anyone knowing, he was the guy they called in. He was in and out without issue. Now what the fuck was he doing in this situation?

"Nicky. You know you've cost me a lot."

Gafino paced back and forth, as if preparing for a big speech.

"I can..." Nicky spluttered.

"You can what? Make it up to me? Last time I checked, you didn't have thirty thousand dollars stashed away. Or, maybe, you do? Maybe you still have some of the money that you were meant to bring back to me."

"I didn't do it, Roy. I swear."

"That's not what I heard." Roy cast a glance at Vincent.

Who was this Vincent? This was a guy Jack hadn't seen before incarceration. Then again, Gafino had a lot of people working for him in the city. His face looked as if it had been chiseled from granite. His knuckles tattooed with the word TRIG.

"This is your last chance. What did you do with it?"

Jack could feel his stomach churn. It had been a long time since he'd been in this position. Fights, blood— these were an everyday part of his time behind bars. Fighting to survive was all he'd done for the last four years. This was different. A man unable to fight back; it was common in this world, but not in the one he had just left.

"I told him." The man gestured to Vincent.

Roy tipped his head back, closing his eyes. Jack had seen this movement before. Roy held out his hand. Vincent pulled a white cloth from the inside of his jacket and handed it to Roy. Roy's eyes opened and he unfolded it. Inside was a hammer.

"Please, Roy, I've got kids. I didn't do it."

When a person was about to die, they gave any excuse to live. Family, friends, lovers, money—it was all the same. Pleading for mercy was like grasping at the wind. Mercy didn't exist in this world.

"Shh…" Roy whispered, placing a finger to his lips. "I'm not gonna kill you…immediately."

In one swift motion, he brought the hammer down on Nicky's right knee. Once, twice, and then a third time. The sounds of cracking bone mixed with screams weren't foreign to Jack. He'd heard it many, many times. But this time it affected him. This time, he diverted his gaze. He felt his stomach twist inside and his pulse began to race.

Freddy chuckled, patting him on the arm. "Like old times, eh, Jack?"

Roy handed the bloodied hammer back to Vincent, and proceeded to wipe a splatter of blood from his face and hands. Nicky's eyes were bloodshot, his face a mess of snot, blood, and tears.

"Let's go."

As they left, Roy hollered back to Nicky. "When I return, I expect you to have a different answer."

The sound of cries dissipated. Back upstairs, they resumed their places in the office as if nothing had taken place. Torture, mayhem, and death were routine. Most would faint, piss their pants, or end up in a psych ward if they saw what went down on a day-to-day basis. But to these men it was no different than popping the cork on a bottle of wine.

"So where were we? Oh yes, you were saying…" Roy began.

Telling him that he was planning on walking away from it all had now become even more difficult. After witnessing what they just had, few men would have had the balls to say anything, but few men had been through what Jack had in the past four years.

"I'm taking a break," was how it came out.

Roy arched a brow. "Of course, what, Miami? Bermuda. Wherever you want to go. You've earned it. We'll get back to business once you return." Roy used a cigar cutter to slice the head off a Cohiba. "In fact, here…"

Roy reached into his drawer and tossed him a brick of money. Jack glanced at it, running his thumb over the end. There had to have been several thousand in hundred dollar bills, each one clean and crisp.

"You've earned it."

He paused a moment. "No, I mean permanently."

His eyes lifted slowly, and they both exchanged a cold glance. It was as if someone had turned down the temperature in the room.

Roy scratched at his face and wiped the remainder of a blood splatter from his neck, before bursting into laughter. The others joined in.

"What a guy."

"I'm serious, Roy."

His face went from smiling to sour. "Don't fuck around, Jack. I've got work for you to do."

"Listen, I don't mean for this to come out wrong. But I'm done, Roy."

He stared intently at Jack, as if trying to decode some cryptic message.

"What, we're not good enough for you? You find God or something in that prison?"

"I had a lot of time to think about my future. I need a change."

Roy chuckled to himself. Ambling over to the cabinet, he poured himself another drink.

"Change." He shook his head in amusement. "What do you think you're going to do? Become a lawyer?

Doctor? Oh, hold on a moment, I got it. You're thinking of joining the monastery."

Jack sat silently.

"You're a killer, Jack, plain and simple. There's no changing that."

"Maybe. Perhaps. But I need to find that out for myself, and I'm not going to find it here. All I've ever known is this place."

"So that's it? You just gonna walk?"

"Look, I appreciate all you've done."

"Yes, what I did. Who pulled you out of that shithole of a home? Who put clothes on your back, food in your stomach, gave you a roof over your head? Hey. Who did all that and more? And this is how you repay me?"

"Repay?"

His eyes flared. "You owe me."

"I owe you? I think I've more than paid off anything I owed you sitting in that cell. I could have ratted, but I didn't. Let's not forget why I was there."

Roy threw his glass across the room. It smashed, sending shards all over the floor.

"Are you blaming me? Are you?" Roy pointed at him. "I should fuckin—"

"Boss, we've got company," Vincent said, poking his head into the room.

He nodded, squinting as he held his gaze on Jack.

"We'll continue this later."

"I'm not gonna be here later." Jack rose to his feet.

Roy scowled, adjusted his tie, and stormed out. Jack caught him mumbling to Vincent, asking him how he looked, before they disappeared around the corner.

Jack headed for the door.

"Where you going?" Freddy asked.

"Does it matter?"

Freddy cocked his head to one side.

"To collect my belongings."

4

FREDDY GAVE HIM A RIDE to a quiet suburb ten minutes away. Apartments in the city were for those who distributed narcotics on the streets. Roy never skimped on looking after his own. Homes in quiet neighborhoods were paramount for keeping his entire operation low key. The only reason he had managed to fly under the radar for so long with the FBI was because he paid for everything in cash, kept business and home life separate, and routinely moved his guys around from house to house. Every six months it was like fucking musical chairs. The only person he didn't move was Jack. Jack was never quite sure why. The FBI was the least of his concerns; being bugged and taped by Roy was.

There had been a few instances in the past where he'd found surveillance cameras; one in the radio, the other in a smoke detector. Roy never admitted to it, but rumors had spread among the guys since Harvey, one of Roy's closest confidants, had been snapped talking with police. Roy was on edge, and his whole operation was like a stack of cards, just waiting to be blown down. The thought of staring down a life sentence wasn't appealing, even if Gafino had given him everything he needed.

"Jack Fucking Winchester." Tony rose to his feet with a beer in one hand and a cigarette in the other.

The noise of the New York Yankees playing on the television was already grinding on Jack's nerves. He'd always had a quiet home. It was his sanctuary away from the chaos of the job, one place where he could retreat and feel sane. He glanced around at what remained of his home. A woman in dirty underwear lay unconscious on the couch. Tracks lined her arms.

Tony glanced over at Freddy. "Didn't you tell him?"

"Where's my stuff?"

"It's all boxed up in the basement. Carver had meant to take them over to the new place last weekend."

Jack proceeded down the staircase.

"Hey, you can't go down there."

"Listen, Jack, you can't have this place," Freddy said, following close behind.

In the basement a stack of various-sized brown boxes were squeezed into a corner of the room. Jack began rooting through them, discarding some of them to the side and tossing handfuls of clothing in a pile.

"Careful, Jack, there's C-4 material in a few of those."

He paused for a moment.

"What?" he said slowly.

"We had to use it recently."

"For what? A bank heist?"

Freddy shrugged, face flashing with a look of reluctance to disclose the details.

Jack shook his head. "Actually, I don't even want to know."

"Anyway, what's left is enough to blow up a small army."

"Yeah, well, maybe you should think about keeping it away from my shit."

He tossed one of the open boxes full of plastic explosive blocks near Freddy's feet, knowing full well that without a detonator it wouldn't explode. However, the look of horror on Freddy's face made it obvious that it wasn't clear to him. Jack chuckled to himself. The truth was that you could fire a gun at it or drop it on a hard surface and the box wouldn't go off. It needed extreme heat and a shockwave. Something that only a detonator could provide. And those were always stored in a separate box.

There had only been a very few times Jack had used C-4 in the past. Gafino obtained it from a local demolition crew in the area. There was very little he couldn't get his hands on.

Slowly reaching down into another box, he retrieved a photo frame. He stared at it, wiping the glass surface with the sleeve of his jacket. He was much younger in the photo. It reminded him of a time when his innocence was still intact. Beside him, an older beautiful brunette with emerald eyes clung to his arm.

As he became aware of Freddy closing the gap between them, he slipped the frame under a pair of jeans and placed it with the rest of his belongings. Gathering it all up, he stuffed the remainder of his things into a green army duffel bag and walked back upstairs.

"Where're the keys?"

"It's not yours anymore; I use it," Tony replied.

Jack squeezed his eyes closed, a band of pressure forming around his skull.

"The keys," Jack repeated, his arm outstretched.

Tony shook his head; he knew better than to argue with him. He ambled back into the kitchen and then tossed them at his feet. Jack scooped them up. Heading out back, Tony followed continuing his verbal diarrhea.

"You know, Jack, you always thought you were hot shit. Well things have changed. You ain't shit now. You're not in charge, Vincent is. You are on the bottom rung, my friend, and…"

Jack paid no attention to his asinine rambling as he

approached a separate garage. He pulled at a handle and the rusted metal creaked up, light flooding into the double space. There was his baby: a black, 1967 Chevy Impala, V-8 with hardtop. It was one of the first things he'd bought. It was his pride and joy. He scanned the surface from front to back, looking for any damage. He'd seen the way Tony "The Lunatic" Marlon lived his life. His lack of attention to detail, inability for showing mercy, or consideration for anything had earned him his name. To think he'd had his grimy hands all over his property was disconcerting, to say the least.

Satisfied that it was still in one piece, Jack tossed his duffel bag onto the leather passenger seat before sliding behind the wheel. Turning over the key, the engine came to life with a loud roar. Easing the car outside, he let it idle while he got out to close the garage. Turning back toward the car, he let out two short whistles. When there was no response, he did it again.

"Where's Apollo?"

"The hairball?" Tony asked, chugging back on his beer.

Jack glared at him.

"Alright, he's at the local pound, probably euthanized by now. Yeah, fucking animal protection showed up here a few weeks after you went inside."

Tony glanced at the neighbor's house. A woman

peeked out from behind curtains. Tony tossed his beer in her direction. Glass smashed. Beer drained out, leaving a small puddle on the asphalt.

"Yeah, you better fucking stay inside."

"Animal protection?"

"Yeah, your dog wouldn't shut the fuck up. Kept barking all the goddam time."

Jack closed the door on his car. Tony, full of liquid courage, squared up to him and then pulled back his shirt to show a wrist that was chewed up. His skin was leathered with scars and looked nasty.

"He's lucky I didn't put a fucking bullet in his head, for doing this."

Jack glanced at Freddy, who knew all too well what Apollo had meant to Jack.

"Now, Jack. Let's keep—" Freddy said, stepping forward.

Jack began to chuckle under his breath and patted Tony on the shoulder.

"Nothing worse than someone who just won't shut the fuck up, huh, Tony? Oh no. I hear you man."

Tony's shoulders relaxed, assuming Jack was cool with it. Dropping his guard gave Jack more than enough time to deliver what came next. Snarling, he delivered two sharp blows to the man's nose with the palm of his hand. His nose burst like a fire hydrant. As Tony collapsed to his knees, groaning in agony and choking on his blood, Jack shot Freddy a look. His face made it clear that if Freddy was smart, he wouldn't intervene. Satisfied that he wasn't going to do anything, Jack returned to his car. Tony screamed at him, his hands cupping his bloodied face.

"What the fu—what the fuck?" Tony stumbled over his words.

He spat crimson red, while an excessive amount of blood dripped from his face.

"You're lucky I didn't put a bullet in your head," Jack replied before sliding behind the wheel and driving away.

5

THE LOCAL POUND was a twenty-minute drive. Jack had gotten Apollo when he was a pup. A Siberian husky, his eyes were a pale blue, his coat black and white. He'd been the only constant thing in Jack's life over the years. While women came and went, friends were buried or locked up, his dog gave him something no one else could: fierce loyalty. That dog had taught him more about loyalty than fifteen years with Gafino ever had. The real kind came with no strings attached. He knew that dog would have taken a bullet for him. There was rarely a moment of the day that went by that he hadn't had him at his side. Heading to the pound, he knew it was a shot in the dark as to whether his friend was still alive. Years had passed. Dogs didn't last long in shelters, with the continual influx, and few people were willing to take on an older dog. The odds were stacked against him.

The sounds of barking and the steel fencing reminded

him of the prison. Every day was chaos. Men acted like caged animals. Few would ever understand what life was like on the inside. It wasn't just the danger that threatened your every waking hour. It was the routine that could break a man. You slept, ate, and took a shit when they said. Human rights activists would have had a heyday if they really saw what went on behind those gates.

If the general population didn't drive you insane, being thrown in solitary confinement would. Men slashed their skin, overflowed toilets, and shoved their own feces under the steel doors. Rage at the warden was common, suicide even more so. There was a reason why men didn't act civilized when they got out. Heck, animals in shelters were treated better.

Inside the building, a gray-haired lady wearing blue scrubs manned the front desk.

"Can I help you?"

"Yeah, four years ago a male Siberian Husky was brought in here. He's black and white with pale blue eyes."

"Four years ago? Likelihood of the dog being here is slim. I don't recall us having one, but this is just my second day on the job."

She glanced at the black tattoo of a reaper on his arm, arched an eyebrow, and tapped her keyboard.

"Do you recall why he would have been brought in?"

"Abuse." The very thought made him want to go back and finish Tony off.

The lady scrutinized him, and her demeanor changed from warm to cold instantly, as if assuming that he'd be responsible. A few more taps on the keyboard and she shook her head.

"Doesn't appear to be any record."

"Can I take a look around?"

"There is no husky on site."

"Well would you have an idea if someone adopted the dog?"

"If we have that information, it's private."

He nodded. She scrutinized him. This was going nowhere fast. He tapped the desk and was about to exit when someone else spoke from behind.

"Black and white with pale blue eyes, you say?"

Jack turned to see a worker bringing in a muzzled Rottweiler from a side door.

"Yeah."

"I remember the dog. Was in a state when I brought it in. They had to perform surgery. That guy really did a number on that poor thing."

Jack clenched his jaw. The man handed the dog to another assistant.

"I believe Sandra took him in."

A wave of relief flooded his being.

"Who?"

"Sandra. She works here. She brings him on her shifts. She'll be in at seven o'clock, if you want to swing by."

Jack nodded. "I'll do that."

6

A FEW MINUTES LATER he was on the road, and a half hour after that he was in the parking lot of the East Star Behavioral Treatment Center. Inside, he was directed to the family common area. With only fifteen other people in the room, it was filled to capacity. Barred windows let in warm bands of summer light. At the far side of the room, staring out a pane of glass, a girl with straight blonde hair that reached to the lower part of her back stood, motionless. Even as he approached, she didn't move a muscle.

"Hey, sis," he said, glancing at her before following her gaze to the courtyard below. A flock of birds broke in the trees. Orderlies clothed in all white assisted disoriented patients around them.

She never replied. He looked at the lines on the inside of her arms. There was more than what he remembered. Surveying the room, he noted how decayed everything was. The place couldn't have been updated for more than thirty years. The sound of chatter blended with clanking water pipes. Paint peeled from the walls and some of the ceiling tiles bore the signs of dried water stains. Whether it was private or state assisted living for the mentally challenged, they charged outrageous amounts—but for what? The place was a shithole and in desperate need of a complete overhaul.

He hated the fact that his sister was here. If he thought she could cope, he would have pulled her out by now. The reality was, though, that he wasn't in a place to look after her. Despite all its flaws, at least here she could receive the treatment she needed. He'd thought of getting her transferred to a better facility, but it had been a long time since he'd had money to throw around.

Jack spent the next hour sitting quietly with her. Though he knew she wasn't tuned into reality, he spoke to her as if she was. He believed that one day she would recover, snap out of it, or at least remember who he was. It was a thin sliver of hope, but he clung to it.

***

Leaving the facility was always difficult. Time with his sister only reminded him of the horrors of his youth, but he was all she had. Returning to his car, he saw Gafino waiting for him. A black Lexus was parked beside his. Vincent leaned against the hood of the car, a look of defiance on his face. Drawing closer, the rear-tinted window slid half way down.

"Get in, Jack," Gafino said.

He didn't hesitate. Wisdom told him otherwise. Inside it was like entering a gas chamber. Gafino's cigar filled the pocket of air with thick, pungent smoke.

"Was busting up Tony's nose really necessary?"

"He got off lightly."

Gafino tapped ash into a tray in front of him. "You remember that kid, Mickey Weatherstone? The kid you knocked out in the first round."

"Long time ago, but yeah."

"What was that? Under two minutes?"

"Sixteen seconds."

Gafino coughed while laughing. "Yeah. First fight. That's when I knew you had something, Jack. I'd seen a lot kids step in that ring, but they didn't have that..." He searched for the words. "That killer instinct you had. You were hungry."

"Angry, you mean?"

"Hungry, angry. It's all the same. You didn't care what the odds were, or who we threw in the ring with you. They were just one more obstacle standing in your way."

"What do you want, Roy?"

Gafino stared at him studying his face.

"What's going on with you, Jack? Look at you. You

look like death warmed up."

Jack diverted his gaze away from Gafino. His eyes turned to Vincent, who was looking off toward the facility.

"What happened inside?" Gafino continued.

"You know there's not much to do inside except think, Roy," he said, pausing to reflect on the past. "Everything. It all plays back. The faces, the names, the blood."

Gafino took a deep breath. "We did what was necessary."

"Maybe. But I'm the one that has had to live with that. And it's all I see."

For a moment they sat in silence.

"Did you get your dog back?"

"I'm working on it."

"Talking about work—I've given some thought to what you said. I may not understand why, but I can respect your decision; so this is what's going to happen. You are going to do one last job for me."

"I said…" Jack muttered.

"I know what you fucking said," Gafino stared at him, raising his voice. "And this is what I'm saying. You are going to do one last job. Once that's out of the way, you can do whatever the hell you like."

"Roy, I can't."

Roy turned, and in an instant slammed Jack's face

against the window.

"You know how much you owe me? I've killed people for less. You screwed up, Jack, and now you are going to clean up your mess. Are we clear?"

Jack motioned ever so slightly.

Roy released his grip on his skull, then readjusted the collar of Jack's jacket as if he was a parent preparing to send a kid out to school for the first time. The guy was like Jekyll and Hyde. Nice one minute and liable to end your life the next.

"How's your sister?"

And like that, he was back to acting as if nothing had happened.

"Same."

Roy nodded, blowing out a puff of smoke. "Vincent will give you the details. Go. Get out."

Jack got out. Vincent handed him a folder, offering a smirk at the same time.

"And if things go sour?"

Through the partially open window Roy replied, "Well, they don't call you 'The Butcher' for nothing, now do they?" Roy narrowed his eyes. "No loose ends this time."

Jack nodded.

"Oh, and Jack, in case you have second thoughts. Maybe one of us will pay your sister a visit next time."

Jack scowled as the window slid up, and the car crawled away.

Four years had changed a lot between them, or maybe not. Maybe only now could he see that he was nothing more than a pawn in a game, an expendable commodity that existed only to meet the current needs of ruthless men.

7

LATER THAT EVENING, Jack pulled into the pound's parking lot and sat waiting for Sandra's shift to begin. Darkness embraced his car, and the only light came from a faint flicker of stars that punctured the sky. Waiting, he flicked the dome light on and leafed through the folder. The address—that was all he needed to know at this point. The rest was routine. Every job was same; the only difference was how a person begged for their life. His job for Gafino was simple. He collected on debts owed. "Protection money" is what they called it on the streets, though Gafino saw it as his own form of tax. You paid, whether you liked it or not. Everyone owed. No payment. No fingers, legs, or in some cases, no existence. He wasn't proud of what he'd done. Killing a person changed you. Despite the lives he took, he had one rule: no women or children.

Light caught his eye in his rearview mirror as

headlights bounced into the parking lot. This had to be her. Jack got out and squinted into the darkness. As two red lights went out, it was followed by the creak of a truck door opening, a female voice, and a dog panting.

"Let's go."

Floodlights at the front of the pound automatically came on as they walked across the gravel.

Jack whistled twice and the dog turned and bolted toward him. Jumping, spinning, whining with excitement, his realization overwhelmed him.

"Hey, boy," Jack said, leaning down and cupping his face. "Miss me?"

"Excuse me, do you know this dog?"

"You could say that. I'm here to pick him up."

"Are you the one who injured the dog?"

"Hell no, I'm his owner."

"Well I'm going need to see some proof."

"Isn't this proof enough?"

"Formality."

Jack flashed his driver's license.

"No, I mean—"

"I don't have anything else."

"Surely you registered the dog?"

What fucking planet was this lady on?

"Lady, I've barely been out of the clink twenty-four hours, I haven't got laid, haven't eaten, and I've had one of the worst days—so unless you plan to call the cops, you're going to have to take my word on this."

Turning to open the door on his car, he heard the familiar sound of a gun being cocked.

"Sorry, but I've taken care of that dog for the past four years, and I have no clue who you are. Who's to say you aren't the same guy who put this dog in here?"

Was this woman for real?

Moving faster than she could respond, Jack twisted her wrist and unarmed her. He released the clip, pocketed it, and handed the tiny handgun back to her. Unable to comprehend how the table had been turned, the woman stood there dumbfounded.

"I appreciate all you've done, but I'm taking my dog."

Keeping an eye on the woman, he motioned to the open door. Apollo jumped in, looking pleased with the outcome.

"Look, here's some money for your trouble." He handed her a wad of notes and then slipped into his car, gave one final nod, and pulled away.

8

JUST OVER EIGHT HOURS LATER, Jack arrived in Rockland Cove, a small town located on the coast of Maine. Full of Victorian houses, quaint motels, and lobster shacks, it held a beauty that seemed frozen by time itself. As he blew past the welcome sign that read: Population: three thousand, five hundred and sixty, he wondered what it would have been like to grow up there. City life had a way of draining energy out of you, but it was all he'd ever known. The sound of New York cabs honking impatiently, tourists and locals clogging up sidewalks and the ever-present cloud of darkness seeping out of alleys, seedy back joints and strangers' eyes wasn't something you got used to. You lived with it. You endured it and unless you were one of the lucky few who got out, you died in it.

Here, though, the atmosphere felt light. A cool summer breeze blew in the smell of salt from the ocean, a few locals waved to one another, and trouble seemed to be absent. In the early hours of morning, the sun not fully up, yachts bobbed along the glistening harbor and early morning fishermen loaded their boats with traps. The town had all the charm of a New England fishing village. A main square in the downtown was lined with antique stores, art galleries, and beautifully adorned wooden plaques hanging outside gift shops, each one engraved with unique coastal names.

The Impala curled down the steep roads and into a lonely stretch on the outskirts of town. Dense trees lined the roadside, shifting from oaks to towering pines as he got closer to the address he was searching for. Soon the leaves would change from the lush emerald-green landscape to reds and yellows. Apollo stuck his head out the window, sucking in the warm morning air and panting hard.

Slowing down to a crawl, Jack pulled over to the edge of the road to observe the place. Nestled in, slightly back from the road, Old Orchard Motel looked as if it was right out of an Alfred Hitchcock movie. Steps led up to a large Victorian house that overlooked a rundown collection of rooms to the right. Outside, various construction materials sat untouched: unopened bags of shingles, a concrete mixer, and heaps of sand. A half-lit neon sign flickered, displaying rooms available, and a rusted Ford pickup truck was parked out front.

Stepping out of the car, he let Apollo out to relieve himself and then poured a bottle of water into a plastic container. As the dog lapped it up, Jack lit a cigarette and grabbed the folder. He'd only had time to get the address, with no further details; he was curious to know who he was dealing with. It was always the who, not the what, that mattered to him in any job. How much they owed made little difference. Why they owed it was what made it interesting. Some jobs were simple. In and out, threaten or kill, but always collect. Others required a little more tact. Depending on the gravity of the situation, he would scout out the target, learn their schedule, and assess the level of risk before deciding on the best course of action. He never rushed in; that was a one-way ticket to an early grave.

Attached to the top of the next page was a photo of the man with a shaved head. A flood of memories: gunfire, a woman screaming, and police storming in flashed through his mind. Matt Grant. His one regret—or as Gafino would say, mistake.

Getting back into the car, he leaned back in his seat and closed his eyes. He hadn't slept since leaving. The car was luxury compared to the bed he'd been given inside lock-up. He wasn't sure how long he'd been asleep, but he awoke to the sound of a storm door creaking open.

Rubbing his eyes, that's when he first caught sight of her. Jack paused. She was attractive. Mid to early thirties? She wore her long, shiny raven hair back in a severe pony. Next to her, carrying a backpack was a young boy; he couldn't have been more than fifteen years old.

He watched as they made their way down the long winding steps to the truck. He gave a short whistle and Apollo jumped back into the car. He waited for them to go by before he followed. Matt was either in the house, or they would lead him to his location. Either way, he was determined to learn their routine.

He followed from a safe distance, letting another car slide in between them. The chances of being noticed were slim, but he wasn't going to take chances. If you dropped your guard for even a moment in this line of work, it could be the last.

The road became narrow as it wound its way around the cove shaped like a U. The beach was pebbled in areas and sandy in others. They passed a white lighthouse and curled down onto the main street. The town was backed up against a vast forest. They passed more boutiques, a small strip mall, and small groups of kids heading toward a high school at the far end of the town, perched up on a hill. He watched them cut into the parking lot. The boy jumped out and his mother waited as he wandered off into the crowd. A few minutes later, she pulled up outside a hair salon.

Satisfied that she wasn't meeting Matt, and thinking that he had a good half hour before she left the salon, he doubled back, hoping to get a better look at the inside of the house. When he returned he pulled up to the front of the house. Dropping the window down to give Apollo plenty of air, he briefly checked the main office. It was locked. There was no note saying when or if they would be back, and no times listed as to when they would be open. It was unusual for a motel in a tourist town.

He cautiously approached the house. Pulling his Glock from behind his back, he twisted a silencer on the end and kept the muzzle low. He ducked into the covering of the forest that surrounded the house and circled to the rear. There was no movement inside; at least from his vantage point. There was no telling where Matt was, or if he had seen him already. It was possible that he was in the shower, watching television, or asleep.

Jack crouched for a moment, trying to make a call on whether to enter or wait until he came out. She'd be back soon. This was likely the only chance he would get. He crept up to the house, thankful that the trees provided much needed cover. Scurrying to the rear of the house, he leaned back against the wall. Straining to hear the sound of anyone inside, he reached for the sliding door.

Unlocked.

He slid back the chamber on his gun and entered.

9

"THERE YOU GO, SWEETHEART. You'll have all the men after you now." Dana stifled a laugh, turning her head from side to side and giving a nod of approval. She'd held off getting her hair done for months. She was so used to it being at the bottom of the totem pole when it came to priorities that it felt good for once to get some TLC.

This year would be different.

The past was behind her, and she planned to keep it that way. It was a new start, even if the tension at home was still present.

"What do I owe you?"

Tonya threw her hand up. "On the house, darling," she said in a thick Jamaican accent.

Dana stood with several notes between her fingers.

"That's what you said last time."

Tonya put a hand on her wide hips. "Put your money

away, and learn to accept."

"Look, I'll pay you back. I'm good for it."

"I know, honey."

Dana gave a crooked smile.

"Now, what have you got planned for the weekend?"

"Besides working?"

"Working? Don't tell me you've filled a room?"

She threw her jacket on, and picked up her bag. "There's meant to be a coachload of players coming through town; thankfully they called my place first."

"Players? You mean the hunky, hot kind that are extensively easy on the eyes?"

"Bowling. Old people."

She grimaced. "For a moment I thought you were in for an interesting weekend."

"Tonya, you are too much."

"Can't blame a girl," she said, sweeping up the hair around the chair.

Dana approached her and gave her a kiss on the side of the cheek.

"Shall I book you in at same time next month?"

"Only if you let me pay," Dana replied.

"Ah, I can't promise anything."

She shook her head. "Go on then."

Tonya was one of the many things she loved about the town. She'd grown up in the area, and with so few people living there, everyone knew each other on a first name basis. People were warm, friendly, and would walk over coals to help you. The past few years had proven that. Tourists from the city visiting her motel would tell her they'd never come across a place like it. Where they came from, everyone owed everyone. Here, they took care of their own. Maybe that's why she'd stuck around so long; that, and the fact that for families it was a great place to raise kids. Even if it had been a long time since she'd felt any sense of family.

Stepping outside, she was greeted by a familiar voice.

"Dana."

"Sheriff," she replied.

**

Inside, Jack cleared each of the rooms on the ground level before making his way to the staircase. The first step creaked and he froze. Worn oak floors. Might as well have been an alarm bell ringing. He readied his gun and ascended. After several intense minutes of peering into each of the rooms, he tucked his weapon into the small of his back, satisfied that the house was empty. In the main bedroom, he picked up a photo frame. Inside it was Matt, the woman, and the kid standing in front of a newer motel sign. Their arms were wrapped around each other, painting a portrait of better days. The walls of the rooms looked freshly painted, and the neon sign fully worked.

He checked the closet. Male clothes still hung inside.

Entering the kid's room, he put a hand to his nose. Its appearance resembled the typical teen room, as well as the odor. There was no masking the stench of old pizza laying on the bedside table. Still, it was a far cry from the cesspool he grew up in. Jack ran his fingers over the strings on a guitar and began rooting through drawers. Under the bed he found a bong. He sniffed. It had been used recently.

Where would you hide, a quarter of a million dollars? There is no way they would have banked that; it would have raised too many eyebrows. He himself would have kept it close. Somewhere where he could grab it and make a run for it, if push came to shove. Opening closet doors, rummaging through bags, running the tips of his fingers along ledges, he coughed as dust fell. He searched suitcases, boxes, bags, and the basement. Nothing. Where the fuck was it?

Back on the landing, he pulled at a cord to the attic. Steel stairs clattered as they slid down. Climbing up into the darkness, the only light came from a large window at the far end, which illuminated the dust, covered boxes, and years of junk.

Great, this was going to take forever.

It smelled musty and historic, like an old vintage typewriter.

At the sound of tires on gravel, he moved to the window.

Shit, she's back, he thought.

He'd hoped it was going to be easy. In and out without anyone getting injured.

***

"Hello?"

Strange. Dana could see a car, but there was no one around. She got closer to the car. As she did, she fell back on her ass, startled by a large dog barking at her. She trembled. She didn't like this one bit.

"Apollo."

A rough and gravelly voice came from the direction of the house. Cupping a hand to shield her eyes, she saw the silhouette of a large man coming down the steps.

"Sorry about the dog; he's actually harmless."

"Could have fooled me."

As he came into view, she stopped squinting. He was tall, broad, and had a sharp jawline with the perfect amount of stubble. His eyes were nearly as blue as his dog's. She noted that for his age, he had a full head of hair: deep brown, thick enough to run fingers through. Holding his hand out, she took a hold, feeling his firm grip. He hauled her up as if she was a feather. She didn't want to stare, but she found herself transfixed. Trying not to gawk, she brushed off the grit.

"What were you doing up there?" she asked, almost forgetting her manners.

"Oh, I wanted a room."

Her eyebrow arched with a good dose of skepticism thrown in.

"Your office was closed…"

She glanced in the direction of the office, then back again.

He thumbed over his shoulder. "I thought someone might be at the house."

"Right. Sorry about that. We don't get a lot of people stopping by here with the new bypass that they've put in."

"Yes, it's a little out of the way."

"We don't allow any animals in the rooms."

"I'll be sure to mention that to Apollo."

She glanced at him, hearing the joking tone in his voice.

"Well, he can tend to drag in the odd bloodied rabbit."

Her eyes widened.

"I'm kidding. He's as good as gold. You won't even know he's here."

She bit her upper lip. She didn't want to cause a scene. There weren't any other guests, so there was no problem there.

"Well, okay, let's get you signed in."

She led him to the office. A wall of heat hit them. The temperature had risen to twice what it was outside, and it was lingering somewhere in the high seventies. Switching on the air conditioning, it let out its usual groan and churned to life, barely offering any relief. It was one of the many things that were desperately in need of replacement, along with the long list of things that had fallen into disrepair.

The man tapped on the unit, and it let out a loud hum.

"Seems like it's on the blink."

"Yes, I'm sorry I can't offer you much in the way of comfort. There are modern lodgings in the town." She paused, watching him look around. "It's actually closer to everything, too," she said.

She couldn't believe she was actually referring potential business to the new inn that had opened up. But in all truth, she still found it a little odd that he hadn't been there already. Few people had booked in at her location over the past year, and those who had were either lost, drug addicts, or had changed their mind once they saw the rooms. As much as she wanted to get the place back to its former state, the expenses were too much. She was fortunate that the motel was paid for in full. That was the one smart action Matt had taken. Where he had managed to come up with the money was another story.

"It's fine," he said, smiling and meeting her eyes.

Okay, hope you enjoy bed mites, she thought.

She pulled out a book from underneath the counter. Inside was a pen. She flipped to a new page, not wanting him to see the large mass of empty pages, revealing how many had stayed in the past year.

"Pleasure or business?"

"What?"

His gaze penetrated her. She felt herself becoming flushed.

"Are you visiting for pleasure or on business?"

"A little of both, I guess."

She watched him sign his name: Jack Winchester.

It was a strong name. She cast her gaze over his muscular frame. It suited him.

"Hopefully more for pleasure," he said, bringing his eyes up to meet hers.

She wondered what he was implying by that. And what type of business was he in? She wasn't into prying. As long as he paid his bill, didn't damage anything, and kept his distance, it was fine.

"How long will you be staying?"

"A few days I think should do it."

An unusual reply, she thought. He didn't sound certain.

There were twelve rooms at the motel. She turned and grabbed the key to room eight. It was the only one that wasn't in a complete state. She kind of felt guilty, knowing there were far better options in the town, but she needed the money and it would give her motivation to work on cleaning up the rooms. Maybe this was the beginning of turning this place around?

"I'll show you to your room."

Not that that he needed directions, but she hadn't been in room eight for weeks and the thought of him running across a cockroach made her even more nervous than he did.

"So you and your husband run the place?"

"It's just me and my son now."

"Oh, he moved out?"

She paused at the door before twisting the key in the lock.

"He's dead."

"I'm sorry."

"Me too."

Entering the darkened room, she spread the curtains wide. Morning light spilled in, the color bringing life, awakening a room that clearly hadn't seen a trace of a polish in many weeks.

"I must apologize." She grabbed a cloth from the washroom and started wiping down the sides of the furniture.

"No need."

"I just wasn't expecting anyone today. In fact, this is all…" she breathed in deep, "a bit of a surprise."

"Look, I have a few errands to run," he said.

"Okay. That would work. I could have the place freshened up by the time you get back."

He moved toward the door.

"If you're going into the town, there's a delicious steakhouse on the corner of Oak and Union. I'm afraid we don't provide a meal here…"

"I will check it out."

He nodded and went out. She watched him climb back into his vehicle from behind the room's curtains. He was handsome, that she was sure of, even if her mental alarm bells were sounding off. Pleasant or not, her gut instinct after he was gone was to go check out the house.

10

AFTER LEAVING THE MOTEL, he immediately phoned Gafino.

"He's dead."

"That was fast."

"Not by me."

Gafino paused for a moment. "Pissed someone else off?"

"I don't know. That's what I got out of his ex."

"And the money?"

"Haven't located it yet."

Jack heard him exhale deeply. "Find out what she knows, and, Jack…find my money."

"You mentioned nothing about there being a woman or kid involved."

"Details."

"Details that you should have mentioned. You know my rule…"

Gafino scoffed on the other end of the line. "A real humanitarian—that's what you are, Jack."

"This changes things."

"It changes nothing. You have a job to do. Do it."

Gafino hung up before he could squeeze another word in. Jack fumed, feeling as if his blood was boiling. He needed an in-road. Some way to figure out what had gone down. It wasn't going to be easy. Bringing up the topic of her dead husband again and drilling her for questions was liable to set off a few red flags, if showing up hadn't already. Maybe her late husband had warned her that men would come.

No, he needed a subtle way to get back into the house. Perhaps the whole empty motel was just a front. With no guests, how could they manage to survive? Maybe they were living off the money, or at least knew where the money was. Most of the time he knew when someone was lying to him, but he couldn't tell if she was. Either way, he would get to the bottom of it.

***

That afternoon, on the way back after grabbing a bite to eat at the Steakhouse, he'd ducked into the local library to see if the local paper had published anything on Matt Grant's death. In a town this size, it was very possible that it could have made front page news if it was murder. That was the question that ate away inside. How did he die?

He kicked himself for not asking, but the last thing he'd wanted to do was give her a reason to keep him at a distance. He shook his head, catching himself thinking about her. It wasn't as if she mattered. This was business, nothing more.

Pulling up an archive of back issue newspapers, he typed in Matt's name. Sure enough, two editions were listed in the search that dated back to over a year ago. A large photo of Matt was positioned beneath a headline that read: Police Search For Missing Man.

Missing?

He was certain she'd said he was dead. He continued reading:

Police are searching for 34-year-old local man who failed to return home after a night out. Matt Grant was last seen at 11:30 p.m. on Sunday when he left The Thistle Inn, on the corner of Oak and Union. Officers are "very concerned," as he has not contacted friends or family. Matt, pictured, is thought to have been wearing a white t-shirt, blue jeans and a red flannel shirt. Anyone with information should contact Rockland Cove County Sheriff's Department at…

He pulled up the next listing. The papers were dated two weeks apart.

The headline read: *Local Man Presumed Dead.*

A vehicle that had been missing since August was pulled from Mill Cove without a body inside on Saturday afternoon after two swimmers found the car.

The Rockland Cove County Sheriff's Department said the car belonged to missing person, Matt Grant. Authorities declined to give any other details about the missing person. The family has asked for privacy at this time.

Jack looked over the top of the computer. There were only six other people in the entire library. Heads bobbed partially above monitors as each did their own research.

If no body was found, maybe he faked his death. Maybe she was covering for him. He ran a hand through his hair and sighed. With so much money at stake, it wouldn't have surprised him if he had gone into hiding with the help of his family. This was getting more complicated by the second. If he was in hiding, the money could be anywhere. He needed more information.

About to leave, his eye caught a familiar face from the morning. Heading out the door with a backpack slung over his shoulder was the kid. What was he doing here? Jack glanced at the clock. It was a little after one in the afternoon. Following from a distance, he watched the boy light a cigarette and hurry across the road, only to duck into a side alley. Rounding a building, he was gone.

For a moment he considered heading back to the car, but when he heard the sounds of kids jeering further down, he opted to go and take a look. The alley began to narrow. Turning the corner at the other end it was his backpack he noticed first, then the three youngsters blocking the kid. He held back for a moment. The ringleader grabbed his bag and threw it on the floor. The kid seemed unfazed. Jack had been in enough fights as a youngster to know when a fight was brewing. The energy was building as the others closed in on him. The kid held his own, stepping forward for his bag, only to watch it get kicked. The ringleader shoved him, leaning in and saying something that he could only imagine. The kid never flinched. But when the next shove came, the kid lashed out at the ringleader, only to be dropped to the ground like a fly.

Jack yelled, "Hey."

Their heads turned. Shock, surprise, or the assumption they were deep in trouble was enough to make them turn and flee.

Bruised, with a slightly cut lip, the young kid hauled himself up and brushed off dirt from his pants.

"You okay, kid?"

He looked at Jack for a split second, grabbed his bag, and replied, "Screw you, man."

He ran off in another direction.

Nice, Jack thought, before turning back to get his car. When he made it back, Apollo was still sitting in the car. The window was cranked all the way down. Jack never had to worry about him taking off. He had sat relaxed until Jack came to the window. His head turned to the side.

"I know, I know. Not exactly the best introduction."

Apollo barked.

"You're right; we need to get some food."

There had always been this back and forth conversation they had with each other, as if they could understand each other with just a look, a word, or a pat on the head. On the outside it probably looked insane, but he cared little about what people thought. Most dog owners understood.

11

THE TOWN SQUARE was called Dock Square. It was located west, toward the mouth of the Rockland Cove River that ran through the town and flowed into the Atlantic Ocean. Despite its small population and the lack of people he saw earlier that morning, the afternoon brought a whole new feel to the town. Tourists browsed the souvenir stores and milled around the art galleries while others filled up small tables outside several seafood restaurants.

Jack took a moment to gather a few personal items to see him through the next couple of days from a local grocery store. Outside he took a seat on a bench and enjoyed the simple pleasure of watching people go by. Apollo lay at his side; his eyebrows went up and down, intrigued by all he saw. Any other dog might have bolted at the first sign of movement, but not him. Jack had taught him from an early age to stick close. A snap of the fingers, one word, or a finger raised was all it took. Jack breathed in the fresh summer air, taking hold of the moment to feel the tranquility of the region. He knew it wouldn't last, but for now he would relish what he could. His time inside Rikers had made him forget how good the simple pleasures of life were: a sunset, eating good food, being able to come and go freely without the worry that another inmate was going to shank him, or simply being with his dog.

His mind drifted back to the task at hand. He didn't imagine it was going to be easy or quick. He needed an in-road into their life, since the idea of holding a gun to their heads broke the one rule he had. The last thing he wanted was to fall back into old self-destructive habits or, even worse, return to jail. In many ways, he wished Matt had been at the house. He would have been in and out. But even then, he was unsure if he could have pulled the trigger. It had been years. And torture—that was completely out of the question. He'd never been one for torture; he left that to Gafino. It was how he got his kicks and struck fear into the hearts of those who entertained thoughts of double crossing him.

Either way, death came with the paycheck, and he was good at it. He'd gained the title "The Butcher of Manhattan" for the sheer number of people he'd killed. Those who knew Gafino, specifically those who owed, knew that if Jack came knocking it wasn't going to end well for them. There was no room for bargaining, even though many had bargained for their lives. Eventually, killing became no different than clocking out at the end of a day.

A flock of birds broke from a batch of trees, providing shade to a cluster of mothers who were enjoying a picnic while their kids zipped around them.

For a while, he imagined what it would be like to finish his days in a town such as Rockland Cove. A place where his past didn't taint his relationships—to live among people who really knew him and weren't afraid of him. Maybe he'd buy a yacht and live on the water. Perhaps even start a part-time business taking tourists out whale watching or offering sailing excursions down the river.

Yeah, a slower pace of life, one dedicated to enjoying each moment that the day brought, and maybe, just maybe, finding warmth in the arms of a woman. Someone he could share his life with, companionship that was honest without the worry of how they would respond to his past. The very thought of being with a woman after being incarcerated for so long—aroused him. In all the rush of getting here he'd barely had a chance to catch a breath, let alone get laid. But it wasn't just about having someone to sleep with; he longed for a deeper connection, one that continued beyond dinner, drinks, and sharing a bed.

Doing that was too easy. He'd spent years of riding that train. It was time for something different; something with a bit more depth, finding someone who would understand.

Cutting deep into his train of thought, the words of Gafino snapped him back into the present. You're a killer, Jack, plain and simple. There's no changing that.

Maybe he was right. Was that it? Was that all he was good for? Surely there had to be hope, redemption for all the wrongs? He wasn't proud of what he had done; the years had taught him how unwise he'd been to hook up with Gafino. Now it seemed only fitting that after being released and given freedom, those closest to him would try to steal that.

No, he had no illusions about Gafino's promise. He knew the man wouldn't let him walk after this job was complete. Of that he was sure. In Gafino's world, when you ceased to be of use, you ceased, period. He was no different. Yet somehow a smidgen of light at the end of a dark tunnel was all he had to cling to. Perhaps the life he daydreamed about beyond bloodshed wasn't just an idealistic fantasy?

Jack cast a glance at Apollo. Apollo returned a gaze that almost seemed to show what he was thinking.

"Let's go, boy."

***

By the time Jack returned to the motel it was late afternoon. The sun had begun to wane behind the trees, as if trying to escape the ominous, dark, brooding clouds that had now moved in from all sides. The evening brought with it a gentle breeze that provided a much needed relief from the heat of the day. Jack paused, his hand on the door to his car, as Apollo jumped out. He cast a glance toward the office where Dana appeared immersed in paperwork. She briefly looked up and swept a strand of hair behind her ear. Her mouth showed a slight smile.

Entering his room, it was almost like night and day compared to his recollection earlier that morning. Gone was the musty smell, the dark bedding, and stain on the carpet. The smell of polish permeated the room. Fresh white sheets and plush covers lined the mattress. The carpet, once damp, was now clean. The curtains were drawn back and draped behind brass hooks. He peered into what had been a grim-looking excuse for a bathroom. It was now spotless, gleaming, and smelled of fragrant pine.

Apollo trailed behind him and began sniffing around the room, exploring every nook. Jack tossed his duffel bag onto the bed and closed the door behind him.

First order of business was a shower. He set a bowl of food down.

After his shower he threw on some clean clothes. He tore apart his weapon and cleaned it while Apollo chewed away at the remainder of his store bought supper. Just as he was about to settle in for the night, he heard voices beyond the window.

At first the noise was low, then it erupted. Moving to the window, he pulled back the curtain ever so slightly. Outside he saw the boy, and Dana.

"Oh, please tell me you have not been fighting again?"

Dana gripped his chin, trying to get a better look until he shrugged her off.

"It's nothing."

"Doesn't look like nothing to me." She paused. "And what's this about school?"

"What?"

"Don't be coy with me. You promised me you wouldn't skip another day."

"And I didn't."

"Then you'll be able to explain why I got another phone call from the principal today?"

He gazed toward the ground. "So I skipped a few classes. I still showed up for some."

"Some is not good enough, Jason."

"Well then what is, Mum? Huh? What do you want to hear? That everything is great now that Dad's not around?

Do you know the amount of flack I have taken over the past year? Do you even listen to the things that people say in this town?"

"It has nothing to do with them. Don't pay any attention to what they say."

"That's easy for you to say, you don't have to face them every day."

She stared at her son in disbelief as he strolled off toward the house. Dropping her eyes to the ground with a deep look of exasperation, she slowly glanced up and noticed Jack looking out. He held her gaze for a moment before she broke the stare and followed her son up to the house.

***

Dana held a phone between her neck and shoulder as she stacked the dishwasher after supper. Her life was multitasking: a nonstop series of to-dos that demanded her attention. Even at seven o'clock her day wasn't done. Jason needed picking up from his friend's house, and she was still negotiating with O'Sullivan Roofing, a local company that had decided not to show up for the past two days. As she listened to another excuse, she wondered what she would give for a night off. A little bit of time away from the drama of life, maybe even the company of a man—but over the past few years that had become almost impossible.

"Patrick, you've been at this for over two weeks. When are you going to finish the work?"

"Sorry, Dana, but I'm going to need that payment."

"I told you I can get it to you next week."

"Listen, I can't get out there anyway until tomorrow, since it looks like we might be in for a bad patch of weather tonight."

"What are you on about? It's been nothing but clear—"

She glanced out the window. What remaining patches of blue from the day were now gone. A light drizzle had already begun to fall. The very sight of it caused her blood pressure to spike and her pulse to race.

"Well, all the more reason to get out here. I'm going to have flooded rooms."

"I can't."

She pursed her lips together, trying her very best not to lose her cool. "Patrick, I have a guest staying right now, and if I don't get shingles on that roof—"

"If you get any leaking, just use the tarps."

"Are you serious?"

"Like I said, I'm sorry, Dana, but I've been called out to several emergencies."

"This is an emergency."

Before she could continue, he interrupted her.

"Hold on, I'm getting a beep on the other line," he said.

JON MILLS

"What?"

It went silent on the other end. Dana blew out her cheeks. A few seconds later Patrick came back on the phone.

"Dana, I've got to go. I'll catch up with you later."

"Wh—"

The call disconnected. She stood speechless, nerves frayed. She really couldn't fault him. The town was too small to hire full-time firefighters. They only had one full-timer and the rest were part-time. Most of them held down other jobs just to pay their bills, and that included Patrick. Had she hired anyone else, the work would have been done by now, but she was doing it as a favor to Sophie.

Sophie was one of her closest friends, next to Tonya. She ran a quaint coffee shop downtown. In an attempt to maintain local businesses and hold onto the town's uniqueness, most of the large chain companies had been prevented from setting up shop in their town. The next largest town, Sandford, was over forty minutes away. Sophie had started dating Patrick a little over seven months ago, and in that time he'd hit a dry patch in his work and she was trying to be helpful.

Problem was Dana hadn't had a clue about his work ethic. There was nothing more that bugged her than someone who promised to get work done and then didn't show up. Sure, he'd been called out to a few legitimate emergencies, but she knew that his heart was not in the job. It was a means to an end; or maybe it was because she had insisted on getting a steep discount due to her own lack of business.

Truth was, Rockland Cove was a hive of activity in the summer and autumn, but over the past few years it had suffered some brutal winters. All the wind sweeping in off the east coast and snow had brought in even fewer travelers over the winter months. That didn't stop the locals from advertising it as a place for all seasons. Of course, those who were insane enough to show up in the off-season usually stayed in one of the newer lodgings in town—those that could offer free Wi-Fi, continental breakfast, and all the cozy amenities she couldn't afford. She honestly wasn't sure how many more months she'd be able to keep the business afloat. If it weren't for the good nature of folk in the town, those who had referred business to her, and dipping into a line of credit, she would have closed up a year ago.

12

SHE COULD HEAR THE RAIN pelting even harder against the windows by the time she'd thrown on her jacket and boots. Finding a hammer and a bucket of nails from the basement, she double-timed it down the concrete steps that were quickly turning into a mini waterfall. She wished Jason hadn't shot off to his friend's house; she could have really used his help.

For the longest time, Jason had been a loner. Throughout his time in school he'd made friends, but either they moved away or lost interest. In recent months he'd made a connection with another kid that kept to himself. He and Luke Evans had something in common, what that was, was anyone's guess. Her father-in-law said they were probably smoking pot. For his sake, she hoped that wasn't it.

Luke was the complete opposite of Jason. He wore black gothic clothing and listened to ear-bleeding music.

The four times he had shown up on their doorstep looking for Jason he was never once without earphones jammed into his ears or gum snapping in his mouth. His appearance was a stark difference to his single mother, Shelly, who was on the board with the town council. She dressed impeccably, and had found it hard to cope since Luke's jerk of a father went off with a younger, much slimmer, tourist. As much as any mother would have recommended not letting him spend so much time with Luke, she knew that approach rarely worked.

Moving quickly across the gravel driveway, she glanced up at the roof, expecting the worst. New shingles covered ten of the twelve rooms that she had available. While her guest was in one of the shingled rooms, she was still worried about the water stain on the carpet. Patrick said there was likely a flashing problem, and the water was still making its way in. He'd said he'd have to tear up the work he'd completed. She felt that was just another excuse to extract more money out of her and keep the job running longer than it should have. But he was adamant that it was because water travels. Either way, it had caused her untold stress, and the thought of losing her only customer was just adding to it.

She tapped on his door. From inside she heard his dog bark, then a rustling sound. When the door cracked open, she could see that he wasn't fully dressed. His shirt was off.

"Oh…um…"

She tried not to stare. He gave a small smirk.

"I hope…um…" She stumbled over her words. "Everything's to your liking?"

He opened the door wider to give her a clear shot of the small metal trashcan taken from the washroom. It was positioned perfectly over the stain. Water dripped slowly down into it, pinging each time it hit.

"Oh God, I'm so sorry. The guy was supposed to have fixed the roofing. I thought by placing you in the shingled one you wouldn't get any issues. But, uh…"

He shrugged. "It's okay, I've been in worse."

Well that was a first, she thought. Her last group of guests complained about everything, and they had been dry.

"Worse?"

Where the heck had he been?

"You want to come in?" he asked.

"Actually I was just about to get some tarps on the roof."

"By yourself?"

She nodded. He glanced past her.

"Where's your son?"

She motioned in the direction of the road, as if it even made any sense. "He's visiting a friend."

He swiveled around. "Well, I'll give you a hand then."

She flung her hands up. "Oh I wouldn't dream of it."

"Listen, I haven't got anything else to do and..." He looked back at the water dripping through.

"No, really, I'll have this done in a jiffy. I'm really sorry about the inconvenience. Once I've checked the other rooms, I'll move you into another."

She took a few steps back and stumbled, feeling even more ridiculous.

"You okay?"

"Yeah." She tried her best to not look like a total buffoon, but she knew that train had left the station.

"Are you sure?"

"Yes. Yes. Go back inside."

He cocked his head with a slight smile, one that she could have looked at for hours. "Alright...if you insist."

***

After checking the other rooms and noting that three of them were leaking—the others were fine, at least for now—Dana hauled up several rolls of plastic tarp left beside the construction material and lugged it over to the far end where the shingles were off. She dumped them on the ground and hurried back, water pouring off her hood, to retrieve a large ladder from the side of the motel. Patrick, of course, had bought the largest ladder known to mankind. It clanged loudly as she dropped it several times; each time she did she noticed her guest watching from his window. He was taking a sip from a cup. Coffee? Tea? Who cared? Her cheeks flushed red from humiliation and the cold.

After managing to get up on the roof without breaking her neck, she began the arduous task of getting the large planks of wood covered. The roof wasn't steep, but coated in water it felt like she was about to slip at any moment. The wind howled, making it virtually impossible to keep the tarp down long enough for Dana to nail the edges down, let alone keep her balance. For every nail she got in, the tarp blew up in her face, almost sending her careening off the roof.

She felt like a surfer fighting against a turbulent wave.

"You know, it would go a lot faster if both of us did it." A voice called out from down below. She peered over, knowing full well who it was. He stood there with his arms wrapped around himself, no coat on. She smirked and gave a short nod. She felt even more embarrassment, but realized he was right.

"Come on down for a moment."

***

Dana stood outside his doorway while he threw a jacket on. With the door ajar she could see his dog, Apollo, staring back at her, as if sizing her up. She wasn't scared of dogs, but this one seemed unpredictable. A few minutes later Jack appeared. She bit down on the side of her lip as they walked in silence. She couldn't believe that it had come to this—getting her only guest to assist her in repairing her motel. Yep, she had officially reached an all-time low.

"I'm Dana, by the way. Dana Grant."

She extended her hand, and he shook it.

"Jack Winchester. But..." He smiled. "You already knew that."

As the gravel crunched beneath their feet, he continued, "Shouldn't the roofer be doing this?"

She threw a hand up. "That's exactly what I said."

"So are you trying to upgrade?"

"Looking to sell."

"So you don't want to keep the business?"

"Can't afford to."

Returning to the spot where she'd positioned the ladder, Jack offered to steady it while she went up, but the idea of a stranger gawking at her ass—even if he was handsome—wasn't something she felt comfortable doing. She insisted that he go up first, and with a smirk in reply she sensed he knew why. Like grappling with a bed sheet, they laid out the tarps and Jack attempted to get a few nails in. She snuck a glance at him as water streamed down his features. He couldn't have been more than thirty-eight, she thought. She'd only turned thirty-six three months ago. His face appeared to show the signs of a life lived beyond his years. She spotted a small scar on his neck, and several on the backs of his hands.

"It must be difficult." He cast a glance at her, continuing to hammer a nail in. "You know, not having your husband around to help out with these kinds of things?"

She was hesitant in her reply. "I guess. He wasn't exactly the sort of man who offered to help."

"Do you mind me asking how he died?"

She scrutinized him. "If you don't mind. It's kind of personal."

"Sure. So what about your son? How's he coping with it all?"

Had he not heard what she just said? "You ask a lot of questions."

"Sorry, I'll keep hammering."

As he took the next swing, he let out a yell and winced in pain while gripping his finger and sliding back on the roof. He steadied himself on the top of the roof with his other hand.

"Shoot. Are you okay?" Dana blurted out.

He grimaced, furiously shaking his hand out. "I'll be fine."

They continued. Once they had the tarp secure, they made their way back down.

"I'll move you into room five; there is no leaking in there."

"You don't need to do that."

"After what I just put you through? Yes, I do." She gave a nod to his hand. "By the way, you're bleeding."

He glanced down to see blood droplets.

"Come, I'll get you all patched up and into a better room."

After she got him keys to room five, Dana led him back to the house. Inside, she took a seat across from him at the kitchen table.

"Nice place you have here."

"Thanks. It could use an update, but its home."

"You know, I could do that," he said as she applied a small adhesive bandage to his finger. "You give this much attention every time you apply a Band-Aid?"

She grinned, taking up the box and placing it back in the cupboard.

"Call it second nature. Lately I seem to be going through boxes of these with my son."

He nodded.

"Can I get you a hot drink? Tea? Coffee?"

"No, I'm good."

"How about something stronger?"

She rifled through her fridge, and pulled out half a bottle of wine.

"Really, I'll pass."

"Well, if you don't mind, I think I will have one."

She grabbed a tall wine glass from the cabinet and poured three fingers worth.

"Listen, I kind of feel bad. There's no fridge or microwave. As you can see, we're in the middle of renovations and…well…" she trailed off. "Look, I usually don't do this, but since you're the only guest here…You are welcome to join us for dinner tomorrow evening up at the house."

He rose to his feet. "Oh, I don't want to intrude."

"You wouldn't; it's just me and my son."

"I shouldn't."

"C'mon, it's my way of saying thank you." She took a deep gulp of her wine, almost finishing it in one go.

He nodded. "You're welcome."

When he turned to leave she added, "Well the offer is there, if you change your mind. We'll be eating at six."

"Thanks." He held up his finger. She cocked her head with a smile. "I'll see myself out."

The door closed behind him and she knocked back the rest of her drink, contemplating what she would tell Jason.

13

THE ATMOSPHERE AT THE MOTEL on Friday morning was vastly different from the night before. For one, he no longer felt like a stranger. Jack woke to the rumble of throaty exhaust pipes. He slowly opened one eye and took in the sight of gold light spilling in through the gap in the curtains. Apollo was already up, scratching at the bottom of the door.

"Okay, okay."

Jack swung his legs over the side of the bed and cleared the sleep from his eyes. He ambled over to the window first, and took a quick glance out. Outside, leaning to one side, were five pristine black Harley Davidson bikes. Each one had been custom sprayed with a reaper on the fuel tanks. Two heavily tattooed men straddled across them; the other three weren't anywhere to be seen. Both of them wore black leather cuts with the phrase Brothers of Mayhem printed in white.

Over the years he'd come across his fair share of bikers. Rikers was full of them doing time for gun running, narcotic distributing, or murder. He understood them while few others might not have. In many ways, they were a lot like the crime families of New York. They looked after their own, pretended to be running legit businesses while behind the scenes they operated illegally. And, like the mob, they were a haven for the lost. Most misunderstood their appeal, but he didn't. It wasn't about acting badass or looking cool. Well, for some it was, and of course on the surface it probably looked that way to everyone. But it was more about comradery and a sense of belonging to something beyond the status quo that held them together. It's what kept them from ratting on each other. In many ways, they were stronger than kin.

He wondered what they were doing here. Maybe they were passing through? Perhaps visiting a friend or family member? Either way, he would have to be even more vigilant. More people on the site meant more prying eyes. He couldn't afford any mistakes. This was already becoming more complicated by the minute.

Apollo gave them a passing glance before going off to relieve himself. Jack pulled out an old packet of cigarettes, half empty. He tapped one out and placed it between his lips. He lit it and tossed the burnt match before taking a deep pull and letting the nicotine hit him.

While he made his usual mental note to give it up, he knew it was pointless. Habits die hard, and this was one he hadn't been able to kick since he was a kid. He threw another sideways glance at the men before looking around and inhaling the fresh morning air. The gravel was still waterlogged, but he knew it wouldn't be long before it was dry; the sun's heat already felt like it would climb again into the high seventies.

He finished his long drag on his cigarette and kept a watchful eye on Apollo. The other three bikers came out of the office, followed by Dana, who made a gesture toward him before leading the men to a room. Jack returned the morning greeting. He again noted how attractive she looked. Fresh faced, and even with little makeup on, she had a natural beauty that radiated. No doubt she caught the attention of men in the town. It had been over a year since the disappearance—or as she put it, the death of her husband—Matt Grant. He'd half expected her to say that she was seeing someone when she mentioned it was just her and her son. He wasn't sure why his mind went there. While he entertained the thought of learning more about her, he didn't want to lose sight of why he was here. It wouldn't be long before Gafino would grill him.

No, tonight he planned on taking every opportunity to pry them for information. In the meantime he needed to dig up more information from the locals. Anyone who knew Matt, anyone who could tell him about the night he vanished. He would need to be careful. It went completely against his usual method of operation, and in a town this small there was a high chance that words whispered could find their way back to Dana—or worse, the police. He'd start with the last known place Matt had been seen: The Thistle Inn, on the corner of Oak and Union.

***

Heading that afternoon to The Thistle Inn, Jack thought back to the first and only time he'd met Matt Grant.

Like most of the narcotics distributed on the streets, Gafino's packages came in from outside the city. Rarely, if ever, did Jack get involved in that segment of the business. The physical danger and risk of being killed or doing time if things went sour were a lot higher than making rounds to businesses who paid for protection. It wasn't a call that Jack made, but Gafino. Gafino left that line of work to men who were expendable. For the most part, Freddy and Louis handled it. They knew what to expect and always met in different locations with multiple exits. Unlike him, they'd seen it all. Undercover feds, greedy distributors, and those who used what they sold. But even his crew could only be in so many places at once. Freddy would handle a deal in one end of the city,

Louis in another, and a few more of his men elsewhere. Looking back, it was clear to see that Gafino's greed and need to dominate the market invited a new line of distributors who hadn't been thoroughly vetted.

Matt Grant was one of them.

He was a wildcard down from the coast of Maine. His enticing offer of an unlimited amount of cocaine was too good for Gafino to pass up. The only problem was, with so many drug deals going down at any given time in the city, it soon became hard to determine which ones delivered one hundred percent pure cocaine. Not everyone tested; some assumed Gafino's reputation alone would prevent them from double crossing him. Those who did, only tested small batches on scene with chemical packs and finger licking, and even then they couldn't determine if an entire batch was completely cocaine without testing it all.

It was a gamble, and a costly one at that.

It wasn't long before Gafino got word that his crew was selling fake cocaine. If it weren't for a cop busting one of the street peddlers, no one would have voiced complaint purely out of fear that Gafino would retaliate against accusations. But busted and thrown against a cruiser, Danny, a kid who handled a neighborhood in the south end, said he saw the cocaine bubble when the officer tested it. Anyone with a lick of sense knew that cocaine didn't bubble. This was the first sign that buyers were being duped and someone was playing a dangerous game. Faced with backlash and a huge loss of revenue, Gafino began clamping down on every deal immediately. They had to find out fast which distributor was cutting or diluting the drugs they were buying. Loads were never large enough to attract attention, but never small enough that they couldn't carry out business for several weeks. Frequency of deals was the key to Gafino staying under the radar.

Once they had narrowed it down to a handful of distributors, it was just a case of determining what to look for. They knew there was all manners of bulking agents being used: baking soda, lactose sugar, and benzocaine powder to name a few. On the surface they mimicked the look and feel of cocaine, but when tested, the product would react differently. They assumed that whoever was duping them was giving them legit cocaine to test and keeping the rest of the fake packages below. The feds were notorious for doing this. It was fair to say that everyone was on edge. There was no way of knowing if they were walking into a sting operation or dealing with a low life just looking to score big.

But with Roy's reputation on the line, the orders were clear. They were to test every package in a load. If any distributor refused, they were to be brought in. Gafino didn't just want them dead; he wanted to toy with them before snuffing out their light. In his mind, what they had done was beyond business; it was personal.

That day was forever ingrained into Jack's memory. He'd chewed it over for years in his cell. What he'd missed, what he should have seen, and how he had managed to escape. Ten days after they had begun checking all transactions, Gafino had asked him to help. Against his better judgment, he agreed. He was assigned to deal with Matt Grant. The exchange was meant to occur in an apartment in the west part of Chinatown. Immediately upon arriving on site, Jack didn't like the look of it one bit. There were only two exits beyond the front entrance; both relied on a fire escape mounted to the side of the building like a black steel snake. Either you went down, or up to the roof and jumped a six-foot gap to the next apartment block. Neither seemed appealing if things turned sour. There was little that frightened Jack, but heights was one of them.

Jack moved in and knocked on apartment twenty-two. An African American with a neck as thick as any man's thigh answered the door, and to anyone else, it would have been a frightening situation. But Jack had scraped knuckles with his fair share of thugs in and outside of the ring. Muscle may have been an indication of strength, but it also signaled weakness in speed. Stepping inside, Jack took a mental note of where the fire escape exit was and the position of the thug. Sitting across the room from them, on a black leather couch, was Matt Grant. With buzzed hair, dark circles around his eyes, and a nervous twitch, he couldn't have weighed more than a buck forty. He had all the signs of someone who was using.

He motioned Jack to take a seat. Spread out on the table were several bags of cocaine, already slit and ready for testing. To the left of him were two suitcases. One was open, displaying packages of cocaine.

"Care to partake?" Matt asked, gesturing to a few lines of white powder.

Jack shook his head.

Matt snorted a line and then wiped his nose with the back of his hand. "Down to business, then."

Jack tossed a few chemical packs on the table.

"Test it."

Matt stared up at him, shrugged, and went through the process that was always done. When he was finished, he asked for the money.

"Test the rest," Jack said.

"What?"

"Gafino wants it all tested."

Jack noticed his hesitancy as he reached over and grabbed a couple of packages.

"All of it."

"That's not the deal. I've shown you it's legit."

"Do we have a problem?" Jack answered.

Matt and the thug by the door exchanged a nervous glance. Jack's eyes darted between them. Matt's motion to grab another package was slow, but it wasn't a package he was going for. Buried beneath the first layer of packages was a handgun. Out the corner of his eye, Jack spotted the thug reach for his own gun. In that instant, firearms unloaded and a hail of bullets shattered the room around them. As the thug dropped, Jack turned back and noticed that Matt had already vanished out of the half open window. The noise of feet clattering up against the steps of the steel ladder made Jack dash to the window. He fell back as a snap of bullets barely missed him. Reluctantly stepping outside, he grimaced, looking ten stories down. With little thought to his own safety he ascended the steps two at a time until he reached the top. He was fully aware that Matt had the advantage, and within a matter of minutes the place would be crawling with cops, but he couldn't let him get away. He fired a few rounds over the edge of the building and clambered quickly over onto the roof's surface. Rolling behind an air vent, he caught sight of Matt double-timing it toward the far side.

He was going to jump.

This guy was as crazy as hell. Hauling himself up, he darted in Matt's direction, raising his gun in hopes he could get a bullet in him before he took the leap. Zeroing in on Matt, he fired once, then again. The first missed and by the time the second one hit him, he was already in a midair vault between buildings. When he landed, Jack heard the sounds of sirens. He watched as Matt limped away, casting a nervous glance over his shoulder before disappearing into the opposite stairwell.

It was the look of fear in the man's eyes that Jack would never forget.

The next thing he knew, two cops were shouting at him to drop the gun and get on the ground. Jack turned, releasing his grip on the weapon and getting into a spread eagle. He spat gravel as they cuffed him.

All things considered, he got off lightly; the thug hadn't died from the gunshot wound and there was only a little amount of real cocaine on scene. Jack got the minimum sentence with the assistance of a dubious lawyer on Gafino's payroll.

***

At The Thistle Inn, he'd spent the first half an hour at the bar observing the comings and goings of locals. The establishment appeared to draw in all types of people, young and old. Some ate, others danced, and a few gathered at the bar. Dimly-lit antique lights illuminated small leather booths filled with families and couples. At the far end of the room there were two pool tables, a cluster of slot machines, and a door that led out to a set of washrooms. In the corner, a colorful retro jukebox played everything from old sixties hits to the modern day noise they called music.

Any number of people might have seen Matt Grant that night. He'd known that if anyone would remember Grant coming in, it would have been the bartender, a fat guy with salt and pepper hair. As conversation flowed, he soon learned his name was Alan Nock, the owner and only bartender at the Inn besides the one that came in on the weekends. At first it was all casual small talk about the area, passing comments as Alan refilled patrons' glasses and wiped down the mahogany bar. Eventually Jack dropped Matt's name. While Alan didn't appear to register what he had said, a middle-aged man wearing a Yankees baseball cap at the far end of the bar had.

The man went from being captivated by the ball game playing on the overhead television to curiously glancing over. After that, Alan began questioning him. Had Jack known him? Jack replied that he was staying at the motel and had heard about the tragedy. The fact that he'd mentioned he was staying there seemed to put the bartender at ease. As for the man at the end of the bar, seeing him later speaking on a cellphone and eyeing Jack nervously was disconcerting—to say the least.

What he had managed to get out of the bartender was

that Matt Grant had frequented the inn most evenings. He was known to play a couple of games of pool with work buddies and enjoy his beer. Alan had seen him chatting with his father that night; nothing that was out of the usual. When asked what he had done for a living, Alan appeared to pretend he didn't hear the question. Instead, he simply ended the conversation by attending to another customer. Jack waited for him to return, but the following hour the man kept himself busy with other patrons and made it painfully obvious that whatever Matt Grant had done for a living, he wasn't going to divulge.

As the afternoon wore on, a group of five men came in and joined the lone man at the far end of the bar. Out the corner of his eye Jack could see them glance over. A few minutes later, they gathered around a pool table. Some might consider what he did next stupidity, but he knew supper with Dana wouldn't exactly be the best place to have a conversation about her dead husband. Indeed, the very thought of it all was confusing. Was Matt dead or in hiding?

Buying a couple pitchers of beer, he had Alan bring them over to the men, following him and introducing himself. There were two things that he knew were true about any man, especially those in small towns. They loved beer and challenges, anything that would transport them out of the mundane. He worked both angles that night. He told them he was only in town for a few nights and he couldn't pass up a chance to rack up a few wins against some locals. Their eyes flared. He could tell it wasn't anger; it was ego. The exact reaction he had wanted to get out of them. The notion that a city boy thought he could take them for a ride was just too good to pass up. They bought it and racked up the table. Jack laid down a twenty-dollar bill. He had no intention of beating them. Hell, he hadn't played a game of pool in over six years. But it would give him the opportunity to fish for answers.

After consuming several pitchers of beer and winning two games, they soon let down their guard and he was able to discover they all worked down at the marina. All of them were involved in different ways down at the harbor, from mechanical services and rentals to lobster fishing. It didn't take them long to get around to his interest in Matt Grant. Jack was nonchalant about it. He mumbled that he'd got chatting with Dana up at the motel, who said that he was dead. In between shots, he mentioned how he felt it was tragic that she had to raise a kid by herself.

"They must miss him down at the Marina," he said.

It just so happened that was where he had worked. According to the guys, he had owned a boat and hauled in large amounts of crab and lobster alongside several of them. It made sense. Already aware that he was distributing narcotics, he had to be getting it in from somewhere. Being a fisherman would have been a perfect cover. Out early in the morning, late in at night. The harbor was only a quarter of a mile from the ocean. No doubt that was how they had been smuggling it in. With this in mind, he used a simple bait and switch tactic of making an assumption about their work in the hopes they would make a slip.

"Must be hard," Jack said, knocking a ball down the corner hole.

"What is?"

"You know, working all those hours for little pay."

Tanked up on liquid courage, few men were able to resist the urge to boast, especially those who would have been making an outrageous amount of money from the cocaine Matt had distributed. The expressions on their faces said it all.

"You'd be surprised at how good the pay is," one of them blurted before another elbowed him, giving him a look of disapproval.

It was enough to confirm his suspicions. None of them stood out as being a leader; they were followers. Town folk who were along for the ride, being led into dangerous waters by the lure of money. But if they weren't behind it, who was? Who was pulling the strings? Who might have had a reason to hide him or kill him? He made a mental note to ask Dana about the boat. Maybe the money was onboard.

It wasn't long before they treated him like one of them, patting him on the back when he missed shots and groaning when he came close to winning. Several times he could have won the games, but he wanted to keep them talking, and money had a way of doing that. He stuck around for one more hour before realizing he wasn't going to get anything more out of them. The one he'd seen initially at the bar clamped down on any questions about what they remembered about that night Matt went missing.

After losing just over a hundred dollars, he dropped his pool cue on the table, bid them farewell, and parted ways.

14

THAT EVENING, Dana sipped on a glass of Chardonnay as she prepared supper. Up from the basement, the clashing of cymbals and the rhythmic beat of drums forced out any trace of peace she had hoped to get that evening. She'd lost track of the number of times she had shouted for Jason to keep it down. The only way it could have been any worse was if his friend, Luke Evans, joined him. Between the beating of drums and the squeal of an out-of-tune electric guitar, she was liable to lose her mind long before the stress of managing the motel would cause it.

For this reason, she didn't hear the knock at the door. It was only for the fact that she turned to refill her glass on the counter that she saw the silhouette of someone through the frosted glass door. She had barely given any thought as to whether or not Jack would show. In fact, she hadn't expected him to. It caught her off guard and for a second she felt a twinge of nervousness in the pit of her stomach; she'd seen the way the bikers had looked suggestively at her. Taking a deep breath, she went to the door and was relieved to see Jack.

"Hello," he said, offering a smile that set her at ease.

"I'm glad you decided to come," she said before peering past him instinctively, checking on the bikes.

"Expecting someone else?"

She gave a smile. "No, I'm…"

She trailed off as her eyes dropped down to the dog beside him.

"Oh, I kind of feel awkward about this, but—hope you don't mind—I've been out most of the day…I didn't want to leave him, you know…I swear he'll be on his best behavior."

"That's fine. C'mon in; I was just in the kitchen."

She stepped back and waved them in. As he stepped forward, she caught the fragrance of his cologne. It smelled piney. It had been a long time since she'd invited a man into her home. Apollo trailed behind him with his nose to the ground.

"Sorry about the noise," she said before hollering down to Jason. "Jason, can you come on up?"

He continued banging away, oblivious. She closed the basement door, trying to seal in the racket.

"Talented lad you have."

She chuckled to herself while taking his coat. "I'm sure he'd be flattered to hear that."

They made their way back into the kitchen, and Dana turned the heat down on the stove. "I hope you like spaghetti?"

"Love it."

She continued browning the meat and then moved over to the fridge to take out some garlic. "Can I get you a glass of wine, or beer, perhaps?"

"Beer sounds good."

She pulled a frosted bottle out and handed it to him. He took a seat at an oak table at the far end of the kitchen; it was laid out with placemats, condiments, and glasses. He thought back to the last time he had been in the house, before he had met her. He remembered that he hadn't lingered long in the kitchen. He'd assumed a large amount of money wouldn't have been stashed in a cookie jar. As she continued chopping up the garlic, he took in the room. Brand new tiled floors, oak cabinets, stainless steel sinks, pans hovering over a marble kitchen island, and cozy lighting made it feel comforting. Despite the aged appearance of the house on the outside, the inside looked modern, as if it had recently been through a renovation. For a second he wondered if that's where the money had gone. Maybe it couldn't be found because they'd sunk it into the home. It was possible. But it didn't make sense. With so many of the rooms in the motel in disrepair, he imagined they would have used it there, if they had used it at all. It was very possible that Matt had funneled it back into the coke business.

"Do you need a hand?"

"No, I'm good. It should be ready in a few minutes."

"You?" a voice said from behind him.

Lost in thought, Jack hadn't noticed Jason walk into the room. He glanced up to see Dana, looking perplexed.

"Jason? Have you met?"

Before he could reply, Jack responded. "Yes, the other day I kind of got lost looking for that steakhouse you had recommended, and he pointed me in the right direction."

The boy squinted, scrutinizing him.

"Oh, that," she frowned. "But what were you doing out of school?"

"It was lunchtime."

She looked at Jack as if to confirm if this was correct, to which he nodded affirmatively. Jason took a seat across from him, clearly looking uncomfortable.

"So you're a drummer."

Jason remained silent.

"Jason, he's asked you a question."

"Well, kind of obvious isn't it? I mean, unless you're deaf."

"Jason," she stammered, giving him a look of

disapproval.

Jack watched Dana cross the room and whisper into his ear. She lifted a finger. "Excuse us for a moment."

Outside the room he could hear their faint conversation.

"What is this?" Jason asked.

"He's a guest. I invited him."

"You never do that."

"Is there a problem, Jason?"

"No."

"Well then show some manners."

As they returned, Jason took his place across from him.

"Sorry about that," she said.

"Not a problem."

Apollo sat by Jack's side, eyeing everyone.

"I noticed you have a dog's bed, but no dog?"

Jason's eyes dropped.

"She went in for surgery," Dana said.

"Is it serious?"

"A tumor. They were going to drain it. They said there really wasn't a lot they could do, except make her a little bit more comfortable and then send her home. She didn't make it out of surgery."

"Sorry to hear that."

"It's Jason who's taken it the hardest. That dog meant everything to him. Didn't she, Jason?"

Jason didn't reply. Instead, he glanced down at Apollo, who was now sniffing at his pant legs.

"You can pet him if you want. He won't bite."

He could see Jason was hesitant. As he petted him, Apollo licked his hand. Jason scratched behind Apollo's ear, and the dog laid down beside him.

"Seems he likes you," Jack said.

"How long have you had him?"

"Six years..." Jack trailed off, recalling how he'd missed out on four of those years while being incarcerated.

"Okay. I think we are ready," Dana said behind a spiral of steam.

***

It didn't take long for Jack to finish off the last of the spaghetti. He scooped at the plate with a chunk of homemade bread. As he did, he realized Dana and Jason were both watching intently. He smiled, wiping his lips with a napkin.

"There's some more bread, if you want?"

"Excuse me, I just haven't tasted a meal like that in...well...I can't even remember. It was delicious."

Dana leaned back in her chair, looking pleased with herself. "Do you have any family?"

"I have a sister. Beside Apollo, I live alone."

"Where's home?" Jason asked inquisitively.

"The city. Jersey."

"You mentioned you were here on business. Do you mind me asking what you do?" Dana said, pouring herself another glass of wine. He could feel his body relax from the second beer. It had been a long time since he'd felt comfortable. The food, the company—it made a change.

Jack hesitated before replying. "I'm in collections."

She laughed. "I thought they did that over the phone."

"The firm I work for prefers I do it in person."

"Debt collection in person?"

"Ah, no. I'm a collector. Antiques mainly."

"Oh." She burst out laughing. "I thought you meant debts. That would be all I need."

He shook his head.

"So you buy pieces?"

"Sort of. They tend to keep me on the road a fair bit."

"You must swing by Maritime Antiques."

"Yes, I planned to," he said.

Jason screeched back his chair as he got up. "I have to get back to my drumming."

He placed his plate on the side.

"Hey it's your turn to clean up."

Jason whined. "Come on, Mum, I told Luke I would have this down by the weekend."

She shook her head. "Go on then," she said, waving him off. "But no more than another hour."

"Maybe you can show me your drums later," Jack added.

Jason paused at the corner for a moment, scanning Jack with an inquisitive eye. "Sure. If you want." He looked genuinely surprised that anyone would show interest.

"Do you play?" Dana asked.

He chuckled. "No, that's one of the many talents I don't possess."

After Jason left, Dana rose from the table and Jack gave her a hand cleaning up the table. He snuck a glance at her. He imagined what it must have been like for Matt. She wasn't only a good cook, but excessively easy on the eyes.

"You don't need to do that," she said as he rinsed the dishes and loaded them into the dishwasher.

"I really don't mind."

They continued talking while she wiped the table down.

"So tell me about your sister."

He went quiet. It wasn't that he didn't have much to say about her, but the thought of opening up to a stranger—it wasn't something he was ready to do. He kept it general.

"Not a lot to say, really. She's a couple of years younger than me."

"What does she do?"

He thought back to what she had been doing when he visited her at the center. Staring into space, her arms showing signs of cuts that had healed over. The look of emptiness in her eyes as if someone had sucked out her soul. She hadn't spoken in years, not since suffering abuse at the hands of their father.

"Jack?"

He realized he'd zoned out. "By the way, thanks for inviting me tonight."

"Oh, right. Well, I'm glad you decided to come."

Dodging her question was abrupt, but the very mention of his sister brought home the realization that he wasn't there to rehash the past. He had a job to do and couldn't lose sight of that.

15

AFTER CLEARING UP, Dana suggested moving to the yard. When he agreed, she grabbed a bottle of red wine and a couple of glasses. They left the kitchen and the noise of drumming. Dana closed the patio door behind her and they took a seat in a pair of pine Adirondack chairs. She ignited the fire pit, and orange flames licked the warm summer air. A crescent moon peeked behind rolling clouds. The sound of wood popping as it burned and summer nights brought back fond memories from happier days with Matt. It had been a long time since she'd sat out here with a man and enjoyed a glass of wine. For a few minutes they both gazed into the fire, mesmerized or searching for words. Dana glanced at his hand and noted there was no ring on his finger or a tan line to indicate he'd taken one off.

"So, do you have a special someone in your life?"

He took a sip from his glass. "No. My work kept me too

busy. It wouldn't have been fair on them."

"Kept you busy?"

"I mean for the past ten years or so, it's been nonstop."

"So you're one of those."

"What?"

"Workaholic?"

The corner of his lip curled up. "I guess. It's not that I wouldn't want a slower pace of life. I just haven't had an opportunity to slow—until recently, that is."

"Recently?"

He glanced at her briefly, then looked off into the fire without replying.

"What about kids?"

"Nope, I somehow skipped that. I'm not sure I would be the best role model."

"Oh no?"

"Being on the road and all." He paused. "But you seem to have done well."

Dana turned her head to the house, where the low sound of drumming could be heard.

"Yeah, he's a good kid. For his sake, I just wish this whole event with Matt had never occurred."

"I'm sure Matt's father must feel the same way," he added.

"If he does, he's tight-lipped about it. He never spent much time with him."

"Strange. Alan at the Thistle Inn made it sound as if they spent a lot of time together."

"What?"

"You know, with his father being one of the last to see him that night—but I guess you knew that."

"Yeah."

She feigned knowing about it, but that wasn't what she had been told. She also found it odd that he would have had a conversation with the barman about Matt. Then again, he was staying at the motel. It's possible Alan brought it up, she thought.

They spent the next hour exchanging stories from their upbringing. At least she did; he listened more than he talked. She could tell he was uncomfortable sharing anything related to his parents. Several times he would answer a question with a question, spinning it back to her. Why? She wasn't sure, but she wasn't going to pry. It was just nice to have some adult company for once.

***

A dim light illuminated the bottom of the wooden steps leading down to the basement. Basements in these old Victorian houses were far from the kind seen in modern style magazines. The ancient stone foundations were exposed, and the area was unfinished. It gave off a musty smell, no doubt from rainwater that had leaked in through fine cracks. At the bottom the basement opened up into a large space, divided by support beams. At the far end, behind a makeshift piece of plexi glass designed to shield the sound of the drums, was Jason. There were no other band members, except a lone microphone stand and an old, beaten up amp that looked as if it had been compiled out of wood from the basement steps.

Within spitting distance of Jason, the noise was deafening. No longer could he distinguish what type of drum he was hitting; it just blurred together as one loud noise that rattled the brain. Jack had never taken up any instruments as a kid. His early years growing up hadn't allowed for the simple pleasures that most kids had. The closest he'd come to discovering if he'd had any talent as a musician lasted all of twenty-four hours. At the age of thirteen he had brought home a Fender Strat with three strings and a missing pickup that he'd bought from a guy at school. Back then, a person could get ten cents each time they returned a can or bottle. After school, he'd go rooting around down back alleys, searching in the trash thrown outside apartments. It wasn't long before he'd managed to squirrel away enough money to pay for a guitar that a kid was selling at his school for fifteen dollars. It was a piece of shit, but he'd earned it and was determined to learn.

Fat chance. The moment his stepmother caught sight of it, she made up some elaborate story that he'd stolen the money from her to pay for it. His father believed her. That guitar lasted all of twenty-four hours before it was smashed and thrown out in the trash. He was grounded for two weeks and couldn't sit down for a week. Jack could still recall the pain as though it had just occurred.

Now seeing Jason beating away on those drums, in some way, gave him satisfaction. While Jason might not have had his father around, Jack would have traded his life for Jason's in a heartbeat. Fathers were overrated, at least in his life.

Jason stopped playing.

"You're really good."

"Thanks," he muttered, giving the impression that he didn't believe Jack's words.

Jason stepped out from behind the set, clutching the sticks. He spun one of them wildly in his hand with all the ease of a pro. Jack peered around, taking in the small amount of personal possessions they had stored there. Several large brown boxes were stacked against the wall. A few dusty suitcases tucked beneath the steps led up to the first floor. A boiler was in the corner. A heavy-duty, worn, black punching bag hung in the center. Jack walked around it. Like most bags, strips of masking tape covered a patch at the side someone had used extensively. He patted it.

"Yours?"

Jason stopped tapping the sticks against his leg. "My father's."

"Was he a boxer?"

He shook his head. "No, he used to work out."

"Did he brawl a lot?"

"A few times."

"Where?"

He didn't reply.

"I'm guessing you don't use it."

"What's that supposed to mean?"

"Oh, I dunno. Maybe the way those guys laid into you the other day."

"There were three of them."

"And? That's just a number."

Jason just stared at him. "Anyway, thanks to you, I'll probably get my ass kicked the next time I see them."

"Maybe not. Come on, I'll show you a few things." Jack slapped the bag.

"Why did you cover for me?" Jason asked.

"Do you like getting in trouble?"

"No."

"Then I saved you some more. Come on, put the sticks down."

He could see some hesitation in the boy before he came over.

"What are you, some kind of fighter?"

"Hit it."

Jason took a swing. The bag barely moved. Jason gripped his hand as if he was in pain.

"Really?" Jack said. "Put your body into it."

Jason tried again, and again. Each time he rubbed his knuckles.

"Forget this shit, man."

"What's up?"

"This is what's up. What is this? Are you trying to bond with me so you can get in the sack with my mother?"

"Is that what you think?"

They stared at each other for a beat. Jason shook his head and disappeared up stairs.

Jack tapped the bag with his fingertips a few more times before glancing around the room and then following him up.

16

AS THE EVENING came to a close, Jack returned to his room and Jason holed himself up in his bedroom, in a foul mood. All attempts at trying to get a word out of him were hopeless, so Dana retreated to the lounge, poured herself another glass of wine, and curled up on the sofa. She spent the next hour on the phone talking to Sophie, who for one was completely disappointed that dinner hadn't ended with Jack and her in the sack.

It was while Sophie was talking her ear off that the sound of loud music kicked in. At first she thought it was Jason.

"Hey, listen, I'll call you back," Dana said, cutting Sophie off in mid-sentence.

After hanging up, she snuck a peek from behind the curtain. She cringed.

"You want me to come?" Jason said, appearing in the doorway.

"No, just stay here."

Outside, Dana made her way down the steps. Her stomach felt as if it was rolling inside. She didn't like confrontations at the best of times, but with five strapping bikers she had considered calling the police. In years gone by, before the whole incident with Matt, she would have phoned him. It wasn't like they hadn't encountered their fair share of drunks, drug-crazed lunatics, and irate customers. But Matt had always been the one to handle it.

The men looked amused at the sight of her trudging their way.

"Do you mind turning it down?" she hollered.

One of them cupped a hand to his ear. The others laughed. She walked a bit closer until she was standing beside the radio. Not waiting for permission, she rolled the dial down several notches.

"Sorry, guys, can you keep it down? We have other guests and it's late."

"Come here, pet, give us a dance."

One of them wrapped his arm around her waist, flipped up the volume of the music, and began swaying. His breath smelt like a dirty sewer. Dana pushed back on his drunken advance; he tripped and fell to the ground. One of the other bikers stumbled over and turned it down slightly.

"Excuse my friend; he's had one too many," he slurred.

With that said, he cut in and tried to repeat the same behavior. Dana tried forcefully pushing him off, but his grip was much tighter. He groped at her ass and licked her neck.

"Get off!" she yelled even louder, but he wouldn't let up.

That was when the music turned off.

"Huh?" the guy cast a look over his shoulder to find Jack there.

"I think you should do what she said."

"Piss off," the biker said, keeping a firm grip on Dana with one arm. With the other, he turned the radio back on.

Jack leaned in, turning off the radio. "I get it. No, I really do. You've had a few beers, smoked a doobie or two, and you're looking to score some ass. You see her; she's got a great ass. But here's the thing."

He gestured to their house, and they followed his line of sight.

"Do you really want to do this in front of her kid?"

One of the bikers lunged at Jack from behind and took hold of his shoulder. Without missing a beat, Jack elbowed the guy in the face, sending him reeling back. The next one launched his attack, but before he was within reach Jack kicked his knee, causing him to buckle in agony. He followed with a crushing upper cut, and the guy went down hard. Another took a swing, but Jack caught his oil-stained fist with his right hand, twisted his arm, and fired a sharp blow into the guy's ribcage. Dropping, he managed to return a blow, but Jack barely registered it. The one still holding Dana tossed her to the side as he threw a punch. Jack ducked out of the way, grabbed the radio, and slammed it against his face. It collapsed the man's nose and sent him down. For a brief moment he had the initial advantage, but then the first biker was back up. He pulled a gun, but before he could raise it Jack moved in one smooth motion, grabbed a knife from his ankle, and flicked it at the biker. It embedded below his shoulder. He stumbled back and the gun went off.

"I'll call the police."

Distracted by Dana's voice, Jack felt two sharp pains in his lower back; dropping to a knee, he grappled and tossed the man over his shoulder. Two more blows to the man's face and he was out cold. Jack had reacted without thinking. It was almost natural, nothing more than years of instinct and pure survival.

Dana dashed into her office and made the call while Jack continued to fight them. One against five; to any other person looking on, it would have looked like pure madness. But to him it was just another day in the yard with inmates trying to shank him. At least these five were unprepared and drunk; injured and exhausted, they groaned, fumbling around on their hands and knees. One threw a hand up to make it clear that he'd had enough. Not taking any chances, Jack pulled his own gun on them while they waited for the police to show.

***

After throwing the men into the back of the cruisers and listening to Dana's side of the story, Sheriff Grant took down Jack's name and details and told him that he would have to give a statement. He made it clear in no uncertain terms that he would be back and not to go anywhere. Five minutes later, blue and red lights blurred into the night, leaving Jack leaning against a rock wall. Jason had made his way down. Dana and Jason looked at him in complete astonishment.

"Holy shit, you think you can teach me how to do that?"

"Jason," Dana reprimanded him.

"What? It was insane."

Maybe it was the adrenaline masking his pain, but only then did he realize what the cause was of the shooting pain in his back. Withdrawing his hand from the small of his back, he saw that it was covered in warm blood. He stumbled forward a little.

Dana gasped. "You need to get to a hospital."

"No. Just patch it up."

"Patch it up? A bruise or a nick on the hand is one thing. But this?"

"Seriously, I've had worse. Just help me up to the house."

His face began to pale. Shock was beginning to set in. There had been countless times he'd got injured over the years. It came with the territory.

***

As they stumbled into the kitchen, Jason cleared the table with one swipe and they carefully laid Jack on his front, peeling off his leather jacket. It looked bad. Blood had soaked through his shirt, covering most of his back.

"Get me a warm towel from the washroom," Dana ordered.

Jason dashed off upstairs while Dana filled a large bowl with some warm water.

"Shoot."

In the entire ruckus, Jack had forgotten that Apollo was still inside his room.

"I need to get Apollo," he said, trying to get up.

"You need to stay put. Jason will handle that."

As she cut away his shirt with scissors, she could see one open stab wound. She washed the wound to get a better look at it. Fortunately, it didn't appear to be too deep; maybe an inch at the most. While this was still shocking, it didn't come close to what else she was observing. All across his back were large scars. The skin almost resembled a dry lakebed with the sheer number of lines. Jason returned with the towels. He ground to a halt. The look on his face at the sight of Jack's back matched her own. Neither one said anything.

Jason used the towels to clean up the blood, and then wrapped the other around him. She knew it was critical to keep a person warm when they went into shock. This was one of the few things Matt had taught her after several of his men had experienced unusual accidents. Tending to his wounds, she thought back to the many times she'd patched up Matt's co-workers. Whenever she asked why they couldn't go to the hospital, he always gave the reason that it was too packed, medical bills cost too much, and, well, he would get this look in his eye. It was the same one she had seen many a time. One that made it clear that anything to do with his line of business or activities outside of work wasn't up for discussion.

"Do you have a handheld mirror?"

"Yeah, um…Jason, in the drawer over there."

Jason retrieved it, and she handed it to Jack.

Awkwardly he held the mirror behind him and glanced over, trying to get a better look at the wound before handing it back to her. Dana shot him a curious look.

"Don't tell me that in addition to being an antiques collector, you're a medic as well as a fighter?"

He handed it back. "Not exactly. But I know what a serious knife wound looks like and what's just a flesh wound."

"A flesh wound?" Jason stifled a laugh. "Look at the amount of blood on your shirt."

"I have thin blood."

"Flesh wound or not, we need to stop the bleeding."

Dana set the bowl on the table and retrieved clean dressings from the cupboard. She applied pressure on the two wounds and taped up three sides.

"There. That should do until we get to the hospital."

"No hospital. I need you to stitch it up."

Her eyebrows rose at the very suggestion. She paused for a moment, contemplating the question alongside every one she wanted to ask, but instead she turned to Jason.

"There's a first aid kit in the bottom drawer, and some surgical stitching in a box underneath my bed."

Jason nodded and dashed off to collect the items. Dana moved to the sink to wash her hands before pulling a bottle of rye whiskey from the refrigerator. When Jason returned, she told him to head off to bed. It was close to eleven at night, and while he didn't have school the next day, she thought he'd seen enough gore for one evening.

She poured herself a glass to steady her hands, and gave the rest of the bottle to Jack. As she worked the thread through his skin she noted that he barely winced; either the alcohol was doing its job, or he was used to experiencing this kind of pain. By the look of his back, he had endured pain far beyond what anyone else had.

"Where did you learn to fight like that?"

"I lived in a rough neighborhood."

***

Ten minutes later she was done. She tossed the bloody rags into the bowl and cleaned up while he observed her handiwork in a tall mirror.

"Why do I get the feeling you've done this before?" he said before taking a gulp from the bottle.

She never replied. He was right. It wasn't the first time she had tended to an injury. At first her need was out of necessity, and then out of fear. For reasons she rarely spoke about, having surgical suture on hand prevented people in the town from talking.

"I guess you're wondering about the scars."

"No."

She feigned disinterest. Without a doubt she was curious, but she barely knew him and time had taught her that it was better to ask few questions. When she returned, she handed him a denim shirt.

"You look about Matt's size."

She took in the sight of his chest and abs. It was solid muscle. He was no overdone fitness type, but it was clear that he took care of his physique. She forced herself to look away, not wishing to make him feel uncomfortable. He took the shirt and slowly slipped into it.

"Thank you."

"It should be me thanking you. What you did tonight..." She paused while washing away the stained water. "That could have turned out a lot worse."

He opened his mouth to say something, but instead continued buttoning up his shirt.

"I'll put you up in the spare room at least for a couple of nights."

"Oh, you don't need to do that. I'll be fine."

"Those bandages will need changing. It's the least I can do."

He seemed to hesitate a moment before nodding in agreement. In all truth, combined with a dose of guilt over everything that had transpired since his arrival, the thought of having him around for a few more nights gave her a sense of security that she hadn't felt in years. She didn't expect the bikers to return, but that didn't prevent thoughts of retribution churning over in her mind.

17

EARLY SUNDAY MORNING, Jack had been up long before the rest of the house. It wasn't because of the pain he'd suffered through a large portion of the night, but purely out of habit. Contrary to what most might have figured, there were only three opportunities to shank or gut another inmate without the use of bribes: first thing in the morning, last thing at night, and in the prison courtyard. All of which meant staying vigilant and surviving on little sleep. He stood on the back porch, smoking a cigarette, as the sun rose slowly. Apollo stretched out on the ground beside him. He enjoyed the quiet; however, the gentle rhythm of the stream among the pines mixed with a chorus of birds did little to alleviate his anxious mind. The sheriff would be showing up soon, fishing for answers, and that was the last thing he needed. The whole situation had become even more complicated. Not knowing where the money was hidden was tricky enough, but having some cop nosing around and running a check on his background wouldn't be good.

He made a quick phone call. Groggy and barely awake, Roy picked up on the other end.

"We've got a situation."

Roy groaned on the other end. Jack brought him up to speed on the events that happened the previous night.

"Shit." Jack heard a match strike on the other end of the line, and Roy exhaled deeply. "This rule of yours, Jack, is getting old fast."

"What did you expect? Let her get raped?"

"I don't give a shit. I don't like this one bit. I expected you to get in and get out. You are getting too close to this."

"I just need a bit more time."

"And the cop?"

"I'll handle it."

He sighed on the other end of the line. "You've got a week, Jack. If you don't find the money…"

"I know."

Gafino didn't need to finish what he was saying. Alarm bells immediately went off in his head. Jack knew all too well what it meant. Roy didn't deal in empty threats. Collections didn't last days and weeks—well, they were unheard of in his trade. Under any other conditions he would have been in and out the very same day he had arrived.

"Morning," a voice from behind him made his heart leap into his throat. Hanging up, Jack turned around to find Dana stepping out onto the porch.

"You should be resting," Dana said.

"I couldn't sleep," he answered with a groan, stretching slowly. "I hope I didn't wake you?"

"No, I guess that makes two of us."

The very mention that she'd been up made him wonder if she'd overheard his conversation.

"Do you mind if I take a look?"

He nodded, holding her gaze. They stepped back inside the kitchen. He undid the buttons on his shirt and she removed it. The sound of tape peeling off and the pull of skin made him wince. She replaced the dressing, stained with dry blood, with a new one. For a moment neither of them said anything as they stood close together. Her eyes occasionally met his.

He decided to break the silence. "How's it look?"

"Ah, just a flesh wound, you'll survive," she said making light of it as he had the night before.

He let out a short laugh that turned into a groan. He slipped his arm back into his shirt while she put on some coffee.

"Why didn't you ask me about the scars?"

She glanced at him over her shoulder as she poured out their drinks. "It's none of my business."

"But you must be curious?"

She placed his cup in front of him and hovered a carton of milk over it. "Milk?"

"No, just black. Thanks."

Taking a seat across from him, she stirred her coffee and added a spoon of sugar. "We've all got our scars, Jack."

Intrigued by what she meant, he was about to follow up with another question when Jason came into the room.

"Morning, son."

He grunted a reply that only teenagers his age would understand. Half-asleep, he ambled his way around the kitchen on autopilot, going through the routine of gathering items for breakfast. Dana took a few more sips of her drink before excusing herself for a moment and stepping out.

Jason slumped down at that table. A bowl in one hand, a cup in the other, he scanned Jack.

"How you feeling?"

"I've felt better."

He nodded affirmatively while shoveling away a heaped spoon of cereal. With his mouth crammed, he continued. "Those were some serious fighting moves you put down on those guys yesterday."

Jack remained silent.

"You think you could teach me?" He paused. "I mean...when you are feeling up to it?"

Gone was the attitude he'd expected from Jason. It seemed to be replaced by a newfound respect. Whether the kid's confidence was misplaced or fueled by a selfish desire to gain, Jack found it amusing.

"Passed the test, have I?"

He tapped the air with his spoon. "Maybe."

Jack snorted as he got up and sat his cup down in the sink.

"So? What do you think?" Jason glanced over with an impish smile.

"I think I need a shower. Keep an eye on Apollo, will ya'?"

Apollo cocked his head to one side. Jason didn't look too impressed, but he gave a reluctant nod.

Leaving the kitchen, Jack made it up a few steps on the staircase when a gust of air blew in. Dana returned, holding a few of his folded clothes in one arm. She handed them off to him, closing the door behind her with her free hand.

"I hope you don't mind; I thought you might need some fresh clothes." She paused. "The others are in the wash."

"Thanks."

"Oh, and there're fresh towels on the rack in the washroom."

***

Half an hour later, a police cruiser pulled up in front of the house. Jack eyed it from the second-story bedroom window. He'd been searching for his handgun, but it was nowhere to be found. He could have sworn he'd left it on the bedside table.

Staring down, he watched the cop climb the stone steps to the front porch. It was the same officer from the night before. He expected the man was back to get that statement. No doubt he'd want to hear Jack's side of the story multiple times before he was satisfied.

The whole event from the previous night had riled him up. He knew all it would take was the cop to dig into his background, and he'd be in trouble. He sighed. Any chance of backing out now was gone. If he ran, he'd spend the rest of his days looking over his shoulder. The thought of returning to Rikers ate away at him. He pushed the thought from his mind; there was no way in hell he'd let that happen. If he went down this time, so would Gafino.

The sound of heavy boots on a hardwood floor, and the crackle of the officer's radio made him weigh his options. In years gone by, before Rikers, in a time when he was a foolish kid, he might have put a bullet in a police officer without hesitation if it meant escaping the law, but now it was meant to be different. That was all behind him, this was all meant to be a fresh start. Meant to be, he scoffed at the thought while cursing Gafino's name under his breath.

About to head downstairs, Jason met him at the door, looking sheepish. He looked nervously behind him before pulling out Jack's gun.

"Sorry I borrowed it."

Jack pulled him into the room, trying to keep his voice to a minimal.

"Don't ever take this. Do you understand?"

Jason looked shaken up. "Yeah, yeah."

Jack pulled the clip out and checked that all the bullets were still there.

"It's not like I haven't used one. Luke and I shoot off rounds all the time from his rifle in the forest out back."

"It doesn't matter. This isn't a toy."

"Like I don't know that."

Jack narrowed his eyes.

"Fine."

"Now be on your way."

Jason ambled back to the door and cut a glance over his shoulder before disappearing down the hall. Jack blew out a deep lungful of air. He tucked the gun under the mattress before heading downstairs.

Conversation in the kitchen was low when he entered. Dana threw him a glance. Seated across from her, nursing a cup of coffee, was the officer.

"Jack, this is Sheriff Grant." She paused. "Matt's father."

He rose to his feet and extended his hand.

Matt's father? Perfect, he thought as he felt the firm handshake.

"Sorry for your loss," were the first words that flew out of his mouth.

"Yeah, well, it's still an open investigation. We'll find him."

The reply struck him as odd. Could Matt's father possibly think he was alive? What part of his disappearance had convinced Dana that he was dead?

"Coffee?" Dana asked.

Jack nodded while slowly taking a seat.

"Were you injured?"

"Oh, no, just a few bruises."

His eyes flicked between her and the sheriff as he waited for the interrogation to begin. There was something he disliked about being in the presence of police. Cities, small towns—it didn't matter. In his early years growing up in Jersey, he had had a clear respect for the badge. At first, like any kid, he'd admired police. As he had grown into his early teen years, he had feared them. By the time he had ran with Gafino's crew, he knew them. The badge meant very little. Dirty cops, that's all he'd ever known. If they weren't on Gafino's payroll, they were working for someone else. Either way, they couldn't be trusted.

"First time in Rockland Cove?"

"Yeah."

"What brings you here?"

And there it was, the question that would lead to a million more.

Out the corner of his eye, he could see Dana watching as the water boiled. Steam spiraled up. She leaned against the counter. Jack was well aware that every word he spoke was under scrutiny. He wasn't sure what Dana had told him already, so he stuck to his original story.

"Business."

"And that would be?"

"He's a collector. Of antiques. Isn't that right, Jack?"

Jack squinted at her before finally nodding. "Yeah."

The sheriff followed his gaze, then looked at Jack again.

"Interesting. Seems an unusual trade for a man of your skill."

Jack noted the way the sheriff didn't break eye contact for even a second. It was what they were trained to do— look for cracks in a facade.

"I'm just glad he was here." Dana added, placing a cup in front of him.

"Who do you work for?"

"I'm independent."

The sheriff took a long pull from his cup. "You must come across a lot of rare and desirable items. What's the most valuable piece you've held in your hands?"

He knew the cop didn't give a rat's ass. It was a test, but one that he was more than prepared to answer. In all his years collecting debts for Gafino, he'd been through his fair share of antique stores, but one in particular came back to him in that moment. The face of a man who refused to pay for protection flashed across his mind. He was the owner of five antique stores spread across the upper north side of New Jersey. He knew he was going to die, which is why he offered his most valuable possession. A rare sculpture made by Pablo Picasso that was worth over seven million dollars. Jack would have taken it and left that day, if it wasn't for what the man did next. Jack had had one foot out the door when the owner took out his frustration on his wife, turning and slapping her repeatedly. Against his better judgment, and even with Freddy telling him to leave it, Jack couldn't. Something snapped in him that day.

"A sculpture by Picasso Pablo."

"How much did it sell for?"

"I don't know. It was dropped."

"Too bad."

"Yeah. Yeah it was." He pushed the thought of the antique owner's bloodied face from his memory.

"Well, let's get this out of the way, shall we? Maybe we can step outside and you can take me through what happened."

Jack nodded, and the sheriff followed him and Dana out.

"So what will happen to them?"

"They'll be charged, put into the court system. No doubt they'll post bail."

"Do we have anything to be worried about?" Dana asked.

"Hopefully not. The court order will take care of that."

"Any idea what they were doing here?" Jack asked.

"According to them, it was a road trip."

"You get many coming through here?"

"No. That's what concerns me."

"Will there be any charges laid against Jack?" Dana asked.

The sheriff shook his head. "For now, no. The men know they are already walking on thin ice. They opted not to press charges. Plus, with you and Jason witnessing the event, you shouldn't have anything to worry about."

"That's good to know," Jack said, glancing at Dana.

"Opting to not press charges, when they were the ones who started it." Dana shook her head.

When they reached the rooms, the sheriff tore off a piece of legal paper from a pad inside a thin metal folder and went through a series of rudimentary questions: the description of the crime scene, who, what, where, and why. He finished by scribbling in Jack's last known address, cell number, and personal details. Jack signed off on it and Grant filed it away.

"Right, that should be it. If I have any further questions, I'll be in touch."

"Thanks, Frank," Dana said.

"Not a problem." He extended his hand once again to Jack. "Well, Jack, I hope this unfortunate incident hasn't put you off our small town. It really is a good location, full of good people."

As he turned to leave, he swiveled back around. "Oh, by the way, eh, how long are you staying?"

"Until the end of the week."

Frank nodded, removed his hat, and slipped into the cruiser.

18

TUESDAY. A couple of days passed without incident. He was still no closer to finding the money or learning what had happened to Matt Grant.

Each time he brought up her husband, Dana would change the subject. His meeting with the sheriff had unnerved him. He'd expected the man to show up at the door any day now after learning about his time inside, but he never came. He notched it up to small town policing. Maybe it was to his advantage.

Once the pain had subsided, Jack had planned on returning to his motel room for the remainder of his stay, but Dana wouldn't have any of it. Maybe it was guilt or appreciation. His stay hadn't exactly been smooth, but they didn't owe him. Heck, if they really knew why he was there, they would have never let him into their house. Each day brought little time to search. Between Dana and Jason he was rarely left alone, and the few times he had been he'd focused on recovering. The past few days had allowed him to heal, observe, and learn their routine. If they were hiding Matt, eventually they'd screw up. Everyone did. A phone number on a pad of paper, a break in routine, or sneaking out for a late night rendezvous were just a few of the careless mistakes he looked for.

For a time, people were good at hiding, laying low and covering their tracks—especially if they knew they would die. He was used to it.

Collecting for Gafino had shown him the lengths that people would go to avoid paying or being caught. Plastic surgery, attempting to leave the country, and faking their own death were just a few of the extremes that people used to avoid staring down a gun barrel. Though usually it was easier than that. He'd once found a man hiding in a makeshift room, in the very house that his wife said he'd gone missing from two weeks prior. Behind a fake wall, they had a bed, television, and fridge. Had they insulated the room, maybe he wouldn't have heard the man. No, collecting on debts was a game of patience. It was vital, and so was using the right bait.

"You want me to do what?" Jason asked.

"Punch me in the face."

"But I thought you were gonna show me how to kick some ass."

Jack snorted. "First you need to learn how to not get

your ass kicked."

He could see Jason was hesitant. "I dunno about this, Jack."

After collecting Jason from school, Dana had gone into town to run a few errands. While Jack was keen to tag along, anything to keep a close eye on her comings and goings, he'd agreed to keep an eye on Jason in the slim chance the bikers returned. Jack thought he'd use this time to try and bond with the kid. He couldn't afford to waste time, but without their trust, he'd be at a dead end. The pair had spent the past hour in the forest, shooting off a few rounds. Jack wasn't keen on the kid playing around with guns, but he thought it was better he knew how to safely handle them than to just come down on him hard over having a natural curiosity. He'd asked him if their neighbors had ever called the cops on them because the sound of shooting. Jason was adamant that it had never happened, since they lived too far from the closest neighbor.

"Shouldn't I be wearing gloves or something?"

"You won't need them."

Apollo curiously looked on as Jack agreed to show Jason a few moves. Above, the sky was as clear as glass; they could only hear the sound of the forest around them and the running stream in the distance.

"Are you going to fight back?"

"No, you're just gonna try and punch me in the face."

"Okay, but you got to promise me—when I knock you on your ass, you won't go nuclear on me."

Jack laughed. "Okay, kid."

The following few minutes, Jack bobbed and weaved as Jason threw jabs and hooks at him. Despite his fragile appearance, the kid had stamina. But, like anyone, he eventually ran out of steam.

"Damn, you are fast."

Jason hunched over, trying to catch his breath.

"You see how I didn't ask you to stop? You stopped because you got tired. Remember, most guys in a brawl will miss shots because they're tired."

"That's it?"

"Of course not. But you've got to know the basics of how to not get hit. Understand?"

Over the following half an hour, Jack led him through the process, tightening up his ability to weave. By the time they were done, sweat poured off the two of them.

"You want a drink?"

"Sure," Jack replied, turning on the house tap outside for Apollo to lap at.

When Jason returned, he handed him a beer. He was holding one himself.

"You're a little young to be drinking?"

He scoffed. "Yeah, I'm sure you were drinking

lemonade at fifteen."

Jack shook his head, amused. Jason leaned back in a wicker chair and stared at the burned remains in the fire pit.

"So you never told me why those kids were hounding you." Jack lit up a cigarette.

"Besides the obvious? They're jerks. You think I can have one?"

Jack raised an eyebrow. "Does your mum know?"

"About them?"

"No, about you smoking."

"Are you kidding? She'd ground my ass for weeks. Now can I get one?"

Beads of water trickled down the side of the beer bottle as Jack took a swig. When Jason saw that he wasn't going to get it, he continued.

"There's a girl."

"What's her name?"

"Chloe. She used to date the meat suit you caught pounding me." He paused to take a drink. "Once she was available, I asked her out."

Jack snorted. "And he didn't like it."

"Exactly. That, and maybe because Kyle still hasn't got over me gluing his pants to his seat back in fifth grade."

"That would do it."

"What about you?" Jason asked.

"Women?"

"No, I mean, have you ever been unable to fight back?" he paused. "I saw those scars."

Jack eyed him as he wiped the sweat from his forehead. He was about to reply when the sound of a vehicle pulling up caused Jason to jump to his feet.

"Shoot. Here," he passed off his unfinished beer to him and headed in the direction of the house. "Let's finish this later."

Jack gave a nod. Apollo lifted his head and blinked before returning to basking in the late afternoon sun.

***

"So you are telling me you had nothing to do with it?"

Jack leaned against the back door, wondering if he should be listening in on the phone call. Uncomfortable, he was about to leave when Dana noticed him and raised a finger.

"I understand, Sheila, but we had an agreement."

Her eyebrows suddenly rose. Whatever they were talking about, the expression on her face said it all.

"You too."

She put the phone down and let out a deep sigh.

"Trouble in paradise?"

"Paradise? I wish. Do you want to go for drinks tonight?"

He was now the one raising an eyebrow. She began

emptying out canned goods from a grocery bag.

"That is…" She stumbled over her words. "Well, unless you don't—"

"Sure."

"Sure?"

"Why not?" he replied.

"I'll tell you why not." Jason interrupted. "Three words. Who's. Cooking. Dinner?"

She scoffed. "I think you are old enough, young man, to whip up something for yourself."

"Like what?"

"Be creative. One night won't kill you."

Jason heaved a few green grapes in his hand and tossed one into his mouth before hopping up on to the side.

"So what is this? A date?" he mumbled, wrestling a few more grapes around in his mouth.

Dana slung him a look indicating that whatever avenue he was planning to head down with that conversation he wasn't going to go any further if he knew what was good for him.

"I think you've said enough." Dana thumbed him out of the room.

A look of embarrassment flushed her cheeks. Jason smirked, leaving the room. Dana glanced back at Jack, continuing to unload another bag. He figured what was going through her mind.

"Sorry, I don't even know why I'm asking you. I just need to get out and forget for one night that I own a motel that is a sinking ship."

"No, I get it. What was that heated phone call about?"

She shot him a hesitant look before responding.

"Forget that, I—"

"No, it's okay." She shrugged. "A large group was supposed to be staying here; it seems they got wind of that little incident with the bikers and decided to book elsewhere."

Jack groaned, sucking air between his teeth.

"Yeah. Well, maybe it's for the best. All those old folks can get super demanding," she said, closing an overhead cabinet.

"Maybe." He forced a smile.

"Look, I'm gonna go clean up. We'll head out in about an hour. Does that sound okay?"

"Yeah, I've got a few things to do."

As she disappeared upstairs, Jack stepped out onto the back porch and made a phone call to the East Star Behavioral Treatment Center. His mind had been awash with thoughts of his sister being harmed, which had plagued his mind since leaving Manhattan. He knew she wasn't safe there, but with little money to set her up elsewhere, he didn't have much choice. Then there was, of course, the small fact that any change in her daily routine was liable to set off alarm bells with Gafino. He'd be watching her; that Jack knew for sure. The last thing he needed was to make him think he wasn't going to complete the job. No, everything had to remain the same. But that didn't alleviate the worry. Instead, he'd made arrangements with an old friend before heading to Rockland Cove.

Eddie Carmine was the only one he trusted, the only one who had stayed clear of crime. He was an old friend of his mother's; some even believed he was Jack's real father. Like any good father, he had warned him countless times about running with Gafino.

He was an ex-marine turned blue collar worker, who could have used his unique skills in service to Gafino or anyone of the crime syndicate, but he chose to spend his years after getting out of the military working at a local factory that manufactured car parts. He was the kind of man who rose early and returned home late. He wasn't afraid of hard work. Never once was he late for work. Nor did he drive. Everything about him was precise. He lived a life of principles gained from his years working for Uncle Sam.

When things got too hot at home as a youngster, and before Gafino took him under his wing, Eddie's place was his retreat. He felt safe there. Eddie always left a key under the doormat, and allowed him to come and go as he pleased. He'd had many a meal at Eddie's home. Had it not been for him, Jack would have gone hungry some nights. Jack thought back to those winning nights when his father and his old lady would drink themselves into a drunken stupor. Those were the worst. He owed a lot to Eddie, and somewhere in the back of his mind, he saw him as the father he'd never had. Maybe that was why he felt he could trust him.

Eddie's was where he had learned how to protect himself.

First it was just a few things, then it became routine.

After getting off the phone with the center, he dialed his friend's number.

"You know, you're going to give your mind whiplash if you continue phoning me. She's okay, Jack."

"I know. Anyone shown up?"

"No. How's it going up where you are?"

"Slow. But I'm getting there. I think."

Eddie sighed on the other end of the phone. "When this is over, Jack. You owe me a beer."

"Cheap debt."

Eddie chuckled on the other end. "Stay safe, kid."

"You too."

After he got off the phone, he stepped back into the kitchen. Jason was downing a tall glass of lemonade.

"Hey, so I tried those series of jabs you taught me on

the bag downstairs. Is it meant to hurt this much?"

Jack glanced at Jason's knuckles and frowned. They were red, and raw.

"How many punches did you throw?"

"Five, maybe ten?"

Jack's eyebrow raised.

"Maybe I'm hitting it wrong?"

Every boxer suffered from bruised knuckles when they started out, but not from a few punches.

"Show me," Jack replied.

Jason led the way, but before they had made it a few steps down toward the basement, Dana called out.

"Jack, if you want to use the shower, it's free now."

He glanced at his watch. "Right. I nearly forgot. Show me later, okay?"

"Sure."

"Oh, and leave the bag for now. Put some ice on those knuckles."

19

THE BUSY BEAN was a café typical of most small coastal towns, relaxed, easygoing, and packed to the walls with visitors. Located on the corner of one of the busiest intersections downtown, it had a small breakfast bar that ran alongside two large windows; each one bathed the L-shaped café in plenty of light by day. In the evenings, small overhead pot lights and modern armchairs gave the whole place a comfortable, upscale feel. Half a dozen round tables dotted the space inside. It was popular among the locals, and anyone visiting from out of town. Most prominently displayed on the front door window were several certificates that detailed awards the establishment had won since opening. It was her claim to fame, Sophie would say. Magazines had recommended it as one of the best places to get coffee on the east coast.

Mellow jazz music played lightly in the background as they entered. There were very few days that Sophie didn't work. It wasn't that she didn't make enough money; she just enjoyed being at the center of the town's gossip. Here, she could overhear all manners of conversations. People didn't visit the local bar in the town to unload their woes; they visited The Busy Bean. Sophie was in many ways like Dear Agony Aunt, a column for relationship advice and a hub for general pearls of wisdom.

No, unlike Dana, her business had only grown in leaps and bounds since day one. Several times she'd offered Dana a job working there. It was tempting to get out from underneath the stress of running her own business; clocking in at nine and leaving at five without any of the worries of day-to-day business would have been a welcome relief. But she wasn't one for taking the easy way out. No, she would get the motel sold first, then take some time to decide what path to take next.

As much as she loved Sophie, even she needed a break from her frequent rants about townsfolk, and more specifically men.

Before Patrick, she had been through a whole line of men. Fat, thin, balding, and even one who wore a wig—something Sophie had only discovered when a waiter accidentally latched onto it when leaning in to recommend the dish of the day. To say she had been horrified would have been to put it mildly. Dana still laughed every time she recounted that night.

Yes, according to Sophie, she had become a connoisseur of the male specimen. Having dated most of the men in Rockland Cove, some would have called her something other than a connoisseur. Dana simply kept her mouth shut when Sophie broke into her usual spiel about having perfected the art of wading through the dross to discover the gems.

Patrick had all the makings of a gem, if he could just perfect his work ethic and finish work on the motel roof.

"Dana!" Sophie waved erratically at them before turning to one of her waitresses to whisper. No doubt she was creating new rumors about Jack, who followed close behind. Sophie was harmless, but she did have a knack of getting herself into trouble.

Sophie double-timed it around the counter, bellowing a few orders to her staff to clear a table in the corner for them. As if she had blinders on, she darted past Dana and extended her hand to Jack.

"Ah, the mystery man who Dana has been talking nonstop about. I'm so glad we have a face for the name."

"Nonstop, eh?" Jack smirked, shooting a quick glance at Dana who mouthed the word, sorry.

"Well, let's get you two love birds...I mean, two lovely..." she trailed off, leading them over to a table as Dana glared at her.

"Quite the spark," Jack said.

"Sorry about her; she's a bit of a wild card."

As they took a seat, Sophie buzzed around them like a bee collecting pollen.

"Okay, so what can I get you?"

"Well, we are going eat out, so—"

"My establishment not good enough?" She smiled. "I'm joking."

"Just coffee, maybe a little dessert. The chocolate cheesecake."

"You got it." She zipped away.

"Dessert before your meal. I like that," Jack said.

"I always think we leave the best things for last. I mean, let's face it; you eat your supper and then have dessert. But by that point you're so darn full you can barely shovel in a few mouthfuls, and yet that's the best part of the meal."

Jack chuckled to himself. Dana traced her finger around the rim of her glass.

"Earlier. When I asked about your sister."

Jack's eyes dropped.

"Forget it, I don't mean to pry," she said.

"She's in a Behavioral Treatment Center."

"Oh."

"Yeah, she had a problem with cutting herself."

"Was it drug related?"

"No. Father related."

She frowned, a look of confusion spreading across her face.

"I mean, she did get involved with drugs, but the cutting, as far as they know, was her way of dealing with suppressed pain. Abuse."

"Oh God, I'm sorry."

"Yeah, not exactly light conversation. I try not to bring it up."

There was awkward silence for a moment. Thankfully, Sophie returned with their orders. Two coffees, a plate with the most insane chocolate cheesecake ever sold on the east coast, and two forks.

"I hope you don't mind eating from one plate."

She had a glint in her eye. Dana knew her well enough to know when she was playing her little matchmaking games. Somewhere inside her head, she had made the assumption that without Matt being around, Dana should be in the thick of the dating scene. It was as if Sophie's mind didn't comprehend that Matt was missing. She assumed he had taken off with a young hussy, and if Dana had a smidgen of sense, she would toss her wedding ring and jump into the sack with the first guy who looked her way.

Dana narrowed her eyes, and that was all it took for Sophie to get the point. However, it didn't stop her from smirking like a Cheshire cat.

"Why do I get the feeling you've had this more than one time?" Jack asked.

"Guilty. Yep, it's my weakness, and Sophie's is the best cheesecake in Rockland Cove. It beats those frozen ones that are full of water. Go on. Have a taste."

Jack scooped a corner of it into his mouth, then nodded.

"Damn, that's something else."

"Good, right?"

"No seriously, it's something else."

He put a napkin to his mouth and removed it.

"What?"

She scooped up a piece.

"I wouldn't do that, if—"

Too late. Dana mowed down on a large section of the cake only to spew it out onto the plate.

"Urgh! What the heck?"

"I told you."

She grimaced as she scanned the room for Sophie. A quick gesture with her hand and Sophie hurried over.

"Isn't it glorious?"

"Glorious? It's mud."

"What?"

Dana pointed to the cake with the tip of her fork.

"Soil, dirt, sod. It's not cheesecake."

Sophie bent at the waist and sniffed it.

"That bitch!" she yelled at the top of her voice. Heads turned before she calmly apologized, and encouraged everyone to continue.

"She did this to get back at me."

"Who?" Dana asked.

"That dirty little redhead hussy."

"You've lost me."

"Monique. I caught her trying to come onto Patrick out back, so I fired her. Patrick thought I was being a little harsh. He said it was harmless flirting."

They both watched her pace back and forth, gripping her white apron with both fists.

"It wasn't the first time. She was always cozying up to him, spending more time talking than cooking out back. I should have seen this coming. Damn it."

"Well…" Dana tried to get a word in edgewise.

"He suggested I let her work until the end of the week, to collect her paycheck, you know? I wanted her gone that day, that moment. I shouldn't have listened. She's the one responsible. I am so sorry. Now I'll have to check all the food. When I get my hands on that slut, I will wring her neck."

"Okay, okay. Calm down, Sophie, it's just a cake. She's gone now. No harm done."

"No harm!" she bellowed again. "What if you had

been a health inspector, or God forbid one of those people who review cafés? Can you imagine? She could have had me closed down."

Dana got up and gripped her friend by the shoulders. She wanted to slap her, but that would have been a tad drastic, even if Dana would have enjoyed it.

"Go back into the kitchen," she mouthed to Sophie, with her back turned to Jack, who now had stepped outside and appeared to be on the phone.

Great! With the mention of his sister, now this happening. The whole night out was starting to take a nosedive into the abyss of despair, and she was pretty sure it was going to be a tough one to crawl out of.

When Jack returned to his seat, Dana hoped her face wasn't showing the embarrassment she was feeling. She took a sip from her coffee, swallowing awkwardness with it.

"Sorry. I had to make a quick phone call." He took a sip from his drink. "Your friend—she's quite a fire cracker, isn't she?"

He smiled and she suddenly felt any sense of weirdness melt.

20

AFTER THEY FINISHED their coffee, Dana made a mental note to swing by Al's antiques. It was only a few stores down. She thought it might offer a distraction from an evening that hadn't exactly begun on the right foot.

She'd been on bad dates before—not that this was a date. She had to keep reminding herself that he was only a friend. More than a year had passed since Matt had been around. She had never entertained the thought that he could have run off with someone else, but now she found herself wondering. Passing several store windows, she glanced briefly at herself, adjusting her hair. She wasn't getting any younger. It wouldn't have been a far stretch of the imagination to assume that he could have met someone in the city. Heck, it could have accounted for why he was such a jerk when he returned. Maybe whoever he had been with had poisoned his mind with dreams of them being together—a life away from responsibility. Maybe the drugs had made him think he was invincible. Who knew? She shook the thoughts from her mind, trying to just enjoy the evening.

The bell above the door let out a shrill sound as they entered.

"Al in?" Dana asked the young kid behind the counter.

"Al!" he hollered out back.

Al Bucklan was in his late seventies. A man who had been in the antiques business as long as, well, some of the antiques in his store. He had flyaway white hair, a thick peppered beard, and a patch over one eye. Being as they were on the coast, most assumed he had been a pirate before he was an antique dealer. Others who knew him knew that he lost the eye in the war.

"Dana, how lovely to see you."

She pursed her lips together, trying to not show her amusement at his greeting.

"Al, I want you to meet a friend. He's in the antiques business as well."

His one eye lit up. "Ah, well, any friend of Dana's is a friend of mine. What neck of the woods are you from?"

"The Big Apple."

He nodded, scanning Jack up and down as if instinctively trying to gauge his worth.

"Well—come, come. Let me give you the tour."

He shuffled his way around a series of large wooden shelves. The place smelled musty, as if it hadn't seen a clean cloth since opening. The walls had been stripped back to the stone, and every nook and cranny overflowed with ancient knick-knacks.

"Impressive place you've got here," Jack said.

"Ah, it's not the nicest—you know, as nice as those other stores—but we carry antiques that will send a shiver up your spine and curl your toes."

He was right. Folks who had lived in Rockland Cove since they were kids knew that Al's store was the first. That was until others moved in and set up shop. He'd never let it bother him. He carried himself with a quiet confidence that seemed to attract people to his store. Dana rarely saw it empty. Al reminded her of a wise old man, the kind that retreated into the forest when they were crippled and grew tired of life and people. But that was never the case with him. Despite his age, it didn't look like anything would slow him down.

"So tell me, Jack. Are you in the buying or selling business?"

"A little of both, but buying more than anything."

"Maybe I can interest you in a few rare items that I don't have out on display. I have contemplated putting them out, but I just can't seem to part with them. The thought of them sitting in some young couple's house and being mauled by a child makes me cringe."

Dana glanced at Jack, who looked as if he was about to object but decided otherwise.

Al led them to a room out back. It looked like a woodworking room, a place for repairs. The smell of oil, dust, and history danced together.

"Now where did I put it?"

He paused for a moment as if to gather his thoughts. The first time she'd met him as a child, he'd been standing so still she'd thought he was a mannequin. She couldn't see his chest rising and falling, or the mischief in his beady eye. It nearly stopped her heart when he moved. Even today, it still gave her the willies.

"Ah, yes."

Pulling out a large box from underneath a workbench, he heaved it up on to the bench. He took out a knife from his top pocket and pierced the thick tape that sealed the edges.

Pulling back the cardboard and sliding his hand into the mounds of white, popcorn-shaped filler, he retrieved an iron statue of a female with a snake coiled around its figure.

"Guess the age?" he said.

Jack hummed and hawed.

"Fifty A.D. Can you believe it?"

"Now where on earth would you get that from, Al?"

Dana asked.

"You are never going to believe this. A yard sale. You know how much I paid?"

"Hundred dollars?"

"Twenty. You know how much this is worth?"

They shook their heads.

"Come on Jack, you should know this."

"I'm a little rusty on Greek artifacts."

"Over three hundred thousand dollars."

"And you never said anything to them?" Dana asked.

"Dana, I'm in business. If they aren't smart enough to figure this out, then they don't deserve to have it." He admired it fondly as if it was some kind of award he'd won.

"So how much are you going to sell it to Jack for?"

Jack raised his hand, but before he could utter a single word, Al had placed it back into the box.

"Nope. I can't do it. It's too valuable."

Dana and Jack looked at each other, exchanging an amused smile. Jack almost looked relieved. They listened to Al mutter to himself as he taped it back up and returned it to the exact spot he'd retrieved it from. Afterward he led them back out.

"You are free to look around the store. Anything else, I'll give you a good deal on. Though anything down in this aisle, here, is off limits. I have buyers coming in from out of state for this. I'm betting it's going to net me a nice little sum."

"Enough to quit, Al?"

"Never. They will have to drag my old bones out of this place."

Dana grinned as Al disappeared out the back again without another word.

"Odd."

"Indeed," Dana said.

"He takes all the trouble to show us, and then opts not to sell."

"You didn't know what it was worth?"

"No. I knew; I just didn't want to steal his limelight."

Jack continued ahead, wandering out of the store.

Dana waited a moment, chewing over his response before following him.

21

A FTER LEAVING Luanne's Lobster Hut, Dana casually suggested walking off the heaviness of the meal by heading down to the shoreline. Misty Beach was a popular spot for folks in the town, offering a boardwalk that ran for seven miles parallel to its beautiful white sand and rockier areas. Tourists and local families flocked there, not just to bathe in the pristine waters, but because of Moor Pier. The pier was a centerpiece that extended nearly five hundred feet out over the Gulf of Maine. At the height of the summer, it was an ocean of faces: hotdog and ice-cream stands, umbrellas, chairs, parents chasing after their kids, and feet covered in sand.

As they walked together, Dana noticed that she had barely thought about Matt over the course of the evening. She also realized that her attraction to Jack had only grown stronger over the past few days. While she hadn't previously contemplated sleeping with him since she barely knew him, the idea had crossed her mind several times over the course of the evening. She was only human, after all, given to desires and needs that hadn't been met in a long time. It had been over a year since she'd seen Matt and many more since she'd felt any sense of love, she told herself. By all accounts, she had resolved that he was dead. Not as way to justify moving on, but as a means to cope.

But at what point did someone move on? Surely it was different for each person. She hadn't been with anyone else besides Matt. That is, except for twice in college, and even then those encounters hadn't exactly been much more than a young girl exploring her sexuality in a drunken binge. Maybe she just didn't think of herself as someone who could just have casual sex. Not that she didn't crave a man's touch. There just hadn't been a time that she could remember where opportunity for it had arisen.

Life's demands had always gotten in the way.

Then again, it wasn't like she was getting any younger. She tried to convince herself that this was how people met. Random strangers. It wasn't much different than those who met someone through a dating site, was it?

She pushed the thought of it all from her mind, trying to keep things in perspective. It was simply dinner. Nothing more. Two people enjoying each other's company. Wasn't it? One thing was for sure: She wasn't much good at discerning the intention of the opposite sex.

Once they had reached the sandy wooden boardwalk, Dana removed her flip-flops to feel grains of sand between her toes. The smell of salt permeated the air. A dark orange stretched across the horizon as they watched the tide rise and fall. Despite it being a warm night, dark clouds moving in from the west looked ominous, threatening bad weather. They passed boutiques, restaurants, and ice cream parlors.

For the most part they had walked in silence, taking in the sights and sounds. She was aware of how comfortable it felt even when they didn't speak, as if there was no urge to fill in the gaps. A cool breeze brushed against her skin, reminding her that it was probably best they didn't stay out too long. Weather changed fast along the coastline. One moment it could be bright and sunny, not a cloud in sight, while the next tourists would dash for their cars holding their jackets above their heads. It was that unpredictability that she liked. There was never a dull moment.

"You cold?" Jack asked her.

"A little."

"Here," he said, taking off his jacket and offering it to her.

She waved him off. "Oh, I couldn't."

"It's a jacket. Not a marriage proposal."

She let out a laugh and allowed him to wrap it loosely around her shoulders. They continued watching the waves kiss the shoreline. Several couples started making their way back, seemingly sensing a change in the weather.

"You don't speak much about your husband."

She dropped her chin. "Not really a lot to say."

He must have picked up on the reservation in the tone of her voice. "Sorry, I didn't mean to pry. It just strikes me as odd that there aren't many photos in the home."

"The few we had are stashed in the attic. After that night, it hurt too much to keep them around."

"Did he and Frank get along?"

"Why do you ask that?"

"The way he spoke about him."

"They...um...had their differences. Matt had earned a reputation for running with the wrong crowd. Frank was always heavy about how his actions carried repercussions that extended beyond him. He knew people talked."

"About what?"

"Do you mind if we don't speak about him? It kind of ruins the evening, and it was going quite well."

"Yeah. Sorry."

There was a moment of silence.

"By the way, that's a nice dress you've got on."

She lifted an eyebrow and returned a smile. "Smooth."

He smirked.

She shivered as a few drops of rain began to fall. Within seconds, they found themselves dashing for cover from a downpour. Having walked a distance from the Lobster Hut, they took shelter below a pavilion. Joining a young Asian couple who were huddled together, they shook the rain from their hair and clothes. The rain pelted down in sheets, turning the boardwalk almost instantly into a shallow, moving stream.

Dana noticed the couple opposite of them couldn't keep their hands off each other. She had to admit it kind of made her feel uncomfortable. She had an urge to tell them to get a room, preferably at her motel. Turning her back to them, she did her best to not listen to their slurping noises. Jack, however, appeared to find it amusing. She eventually found herself seeing the funny side to their situation. Out of all of the pavilions along the seven-mile stretch, they had wound up with two Asian nymphomaniacs.

"Would you mind taking a photo of us?"

Dana turned around to find the young male thrusting his oversized Nikon camera toward her. Thankfully that was the only thing he was thrusting.

"Sure."

After taking the photo she handed it back.

"Would you like me to take a photo of you both?"

Dana screwed up her face as if they would know. "Oh, uh, we're not together."

As she said it, she glanced at Jack, who was already in the process of handing the guy his cellphone.

"For memory's sake. Who knows when I'll be back this way?"

"Okay," she stretched the word out moving toward him yet keeping an acceptable distance. It was then that she caught the scent of his cologne. He smelled good; almost too good. She felt her stomach turn within her. As he wrapped a strong arm around her and brought her in close, her guard dropped. He unnerved her, but she wasn't sure why. It wasn't like he was doing anything that was out of bounds. It was a photo. Get a grip, she told herself. It was just that she was aware of her attraction to him. He wasn't seeing anyone, at least from what he had told her. But the thought of getting drawn into a short-lived fling with a stranger only to never see him again was a disappointment she didn't want to experience. Was he that? A stranger? At what point did a person become more?

After taking the shot and handing back the phone, the young couple must have realized the rain wasn't going to let up. They made a decision to make a dash for it, leaving the two of them standing alone beneath the pavilion, listening to the sound of rain bouncing off the metal roof. Instead of stepping out from under his arm or letting go of his waist, she turned into him.

"Why did you help me?"

His eyes met hers. "You mean with the roof?"

"No, the bikers. Why did you risk getting involved?"

"I don't think I did anything that anyone else wouldn't have."

"No. Most would have called the police. Most would have looked the other way. The way you dealt with them. It's like you had done it before. You were comfortable."

He turned his head. "I wouldn't say I was comfortable. Like I said, I grew up in tough neighborhood."

"So you got into fights a lot?"

"You could say that. I locked heads a few times. Most do."

"So you're a troublemaker?" She smiled.

He smirked. "I know how to handle myself, if that's what you're asking."

"And others?"

"I'm not very good with people."

"No?"

He slowly shook his head. She stepped closer to him, watching his chest rise and fall. Placing a hand on his chest, she could feel his heart beating fast. Noticing a strand of hair stuck to her cheek, he reached up and swept it back behind her ear. His hand cupped the side of her face. His eyes lowered to hers. Ever so slowly, the distance between them closed.

Hesitantly, she leaned in. In that moment her lips pressed against his, his mouth closing over hers. She breathed out fully then moved deeper into his arms. Breaking their kiss, his lip curved up ever so slightly. Approval? With the side of his thumb, he ran his fingers over the side of her cheek. Studying each other's faces, she could feel her pulse quickening before they kissed again. This time it was with more intensity, his hand sliding down the curve of her back.

She'd desired this since dinner. Her eyes ran over his face, watched his lips as they talked, and hung on his every word. And then, as quickly as it had started, it ended. He pulled back.

"I'm sorry, I—" she muttered.

"It's not you. Trust me. It's definitely not you."

"What is it, then?"

He looked away. "We should go."

She was confused. He had kissed her back. She had felt it. Any other man would have taken full advantage of a moment like that. She frowned, trying not to show her frustration or embarrassment. But she couldn't help feeling foolish.

The rain was beginning to let up. What had started as a heavy downpour was now barely registering on her skin. Unable to understand why he had pulled away, she took off his jacket and handed it back to him.

Once they reached her truck, he paused for a moment.

"Listen. I like you, Dana. I really do. There's just some things about me that—"

"You've got baggage. Don't we all?"

"No it's—"

"What, you're married?"

"No."

"Seeing someone?"

He shook his head.

"Didn't you enjoy this evening?"

"Of course."

"Then what's the problem?"

His eyes dropped before meeting hers.

She threw a hand up before hopping in. "Fine. It's your business. I shouldn't have…"

Inside the truck he immediately placed his hand on hers.

"I don't want to end the evening this way."

As much as she felt frustrated, she couldn't fault him for her own misplaced expectations. Reluctantly, she nodded.

"Can I show you something?" she asked.

22

THE SUN HAD DIPPED behind a vast line of old-growth pine trees by the time they made it to Rockland Cove's coastline. It wrapped orange and yellow bands of light around the dangerously sharp rocks that cut into the ocean. Strangely, the light gave off an almost pink appearance. As they reached the mouth of Lighthouse Road, it opened up into a circular parking lot. It was empty, and the asphalt had fallen into disrepair. Dana let the truck idle after placing it into park.

"Be one moment," she said before slamming the door.

Jack observed her physique as she unhooked a lock around a thick rusted chain that bound two steel gates closed. She had curves in all the right places—the kind that could make a man's heart race and unearth a deep sensual craving. The wind whipped at her cascade of dark hair. She swept it out of her face as she swung the gate open. On the way back to the truck, she must have noticed he was looking since she offered the smallest hint of a smile. Casting a glance over her shoulder, satisfied there was enough room to squeeze through, she hopped back in.

"So…" he said slowly. "What you need to show me is out there?" he asked inquisitively.

Beyond the gates were large, flat, granite rocks that extended in a line toward a tiny structure in the distance. They had to have been at least a mile or two from the main land. Like a manmade dock, the breakwater was just wide enough for one vehicle. Either side of that was a collection of jagged rocks, as if the tightrope in the middle and the ocean sloshing around it wasn't unnerving enough.

"Yeah, you're not afraid of a little water, are you?" She smirked, seemingly picking up some reservation in the tone of his voice.

Jack looked out, thinking, as a surge of waves splashed up and over the breakwater. Though he didn't look at her, Jack knew she was still watching him. He feigned confidence and tried not to grimace.

He chuckled. "Are you kidding?" He felt a bead of sweat forming on his brow.

Truth be told, he'd lived his whole life by the eastern shore, and yet in all his time in the city not once had he ridden the ferry over to Staten Island. He'd always given the ocean a wide berth. He had his father to thank for that.

There wasn't anything that caused his heart to pound more than the sight of water. A flashback from his childhood, choking on water and gasping for air, made his chest rise faster. Really, it shouldn't have affected him as much as it did. It's not like his father had attempted to drown him in anything deeper than a bathtub, but regardless, subconsciously a deep seated fear had been instilled in him from the age of seven.

The water glistened against the sun in the distance, its glare almost blinding. Finding it hard to see ahead really didn't help the situation either. He gulped before telling himself to get a grip. It was just water, after all. At the sound of gravel beneath the tires, the truck rolled forward, its movement reminding him of a rollercoaster about to drop over the edge.

As they drew closer to the end of the stone jetty, he could see a large, Victorian lighthouse keeper's house with a red roof and eyebrow porch. Looming behind it was a classic white conical lighthouse tower. In an instant, it was clear that the surrounding grounds hadn't been taken care of in years. Overgrown grass with brown tips, singed by the summer heat wave, needed cutting; tree limbs reached for the earth and shrubs spider-webbed every inch of the rural landscape. Though unkempt and wild, it still held a certain New England charm that could only be found off the beaten path. Butterflies flitted from one flower to the next. Seagulls circled overhead, squawking. Upon a gentle breeze the salty scent of the ocean carried. In every way it was a coastal treasure that time had forgotten.

"You own this property?"

"Yeah, sort of."

"Sort of?"

"The lighthouse portion has been run by the U.S Coastal Guard since '89. It was the last lighthouse in Maine to be automated. The home belonged to my parents. They were keepers until..." she said, trailing off.

He noted the way her chin dropped. He chose not to probe any further.

"Anyway, it's where I come when I want to be alone. I feel safe here."

By the time they stopped near the house, his knuckles were almost white from gripping the door handle. After climbing out of the truck and continuing to take in the scene, he rolled his head around to relieve the tension that had formed at the back of his neck.

A small, winding pathway, barely visible beneath the foliage, led up to the house. Everything about the place was truly breathtaking. It was easy to imagine what it must have been like to live and work in the middle of the ocean, surrounded by endless beauty, a sea of color, and a cloudless sky. And yet how could she feel safe surrounded by this much water? Not every day would be as nice as this. From somewhere in the distance, he heard the faint rumble of thunder, adding to his present fear.

As they made their way up to the porch, the sun bled into the ocean and they could feel the final rays of its warmth against their skin. It would soon be dark. Despite his dislike for the ocean, being with her felt good—right even—as though someone behind the scenes was leading him, guiding his steps. Walking behind her, he wondered again how anyone like her could have wound up with someone like Matt. Then again, his life wasn't much better than Matt's had been. Had Matt had friends forcing him to sell drugs? Had the need of running a motel been too much? He liked to think that behind it all, there was a good reason. If only so he could make sense of his own life choices.

"You don't get out here much?" he said, letting his hand drift through some long reeds that had grown up between the grass.

"It's been a while, with work and everything over the past year. We used to spend a lot of summers here. Weekends, that is, when we had staff to manage the hotel."

"If you sell the motel, will you stay here?"

"That's the plan. I'm not sure when that will be, though. I just know I can't keep up the motel business. It's barely breaking even."

"You've never thought of selling this place?"

She gaped. "No way. It's priceless."

They spent the next few minutes roaming the grounds while Dana pointed out different areas that had meant a lot to her growing up. A broken treehouse her father had built for her and her sister when she was five. The spot where she fell off a tire swing and broke her arm at age nine. A stone well that had been filled in with soil and turned into a small plot for morning glories. She spoke of sneaking out as a kid, exploring the grounds and at one time nearly falling down the well, after which her father filled it in. He observed the way her face lit up and seemed at ease, reliving her youth and remembering a time far from the stress and pain she had endured over the past few years.

"You never told me you had a sister."

"She lives on the west coast. We rarely speak."

"Tell me about it," he muttered under his breath, thinking about his own sister. It had been years since he'd heard her voice.

He was curious, but didn't question her on it. Dana must have read his mind, since she continued.

"She didn't approve of my relationship with Matt.

That is, me staying in it."

Her reply only raised further questions. Did she know about Matt's additional activities? Had she been involved? What had she confided to her sister?

Unlocking the door to the main entrance, Dana flicked on a switch. Light illuminated the short hallway. He could immediately see why this place felt safe. Closing the door behind him, the noise of the wind vanished. The place was built like Fort Knox, but with all the trimmings of a modernized Victorian home. Obviously it had to be able to withstand the severe beatings of Mother Nature. Color photographs lined the walls, holding captive moments in time. Fluffy pillows and throw overs covered furniture. The pine floors had been stripped back and coated with a dark stain. What little light remained of the day seeped in through a large, double paned window that provided a magnificent view of the ocean. The kitchen had an open concept that led into the lounge.

His eyes scanned the scuffed pine floors, brick and mortar walls, and a double barrel shotgun locked in place above the fireplace. A large wrap around bookcase filled with old books, and displaying miniature porcelain dogs, was the focal point of the lounge. Someone was an avid reader and collector. Jack ran his fingers across the leather bound spines.

"Those belonged to my father," she said, tossing her

keys on the counter before lighting the pilot light.

"Coffee?"

"Maybe later."

He imagined what it may have been like to have met her when she was younger, to have grown up in a small town away from a life of crime. Would it have been the same? Not unless he'd had different parents, he thought. A sudden wave of guilt hit him hard, like the waves crashing against the rocks around them. Surrounded by the beauty of nature and sharing each day with Dana since he'd arrived, it was easy to forget why he was here, and all that could mean to her. All that could be lost. Images of the chaos erupting and obliterating what little remaining peace she had flashed before him.

It was the reason he'd pulled away under the pavilion.

He'd never given much thought to how his actions affected others until recently. The past was like a blur in his rearview mirror, a distant series of memories that he preferred to forget or keep hidden.

The thought of leaving once he found the money, or her finding out why he was really there, had begun to pain him more than he anticipated. Almost unknowingly, being around her was changing him. He scoffed. Maybe he was just trying to convince himself that he could be something other than his past. He'd spent so many years ignoring the shame of who he'd become, the lives he'd taken with little regard for those left behind. He'd long ago accepted that the road he had chosen, the choices he had made, didn't deserve a happy outcome.

Then again, a life of crime brought its own penalty.

As the evening wore on, he noticed the way it felt to be around her. There was no denying his attraction to her, and he could now see the feeling was mutual. There was something natural in their interaction. It didn't seem forced, fake, or needy as many of his past relationships and nights with women had been. Conversation flowed, along with laughter. For maybe the first time in his life, he wasn't in a hurry to lose the company. Prior to his incarceration, his life had never allowed for anything deeper than a one-night stand. Of course there were those around him who had family and kids, those who spent weekends tossing burgers on the BBQ and trying to appear normal on the surface, but to him it was all smoke and mirrors.

Normal, he scoffed internally. What was that? A home, a wife, two kids, and having a job you hate? Was that normal? Maybe it was. However, in all his time in the city, he'd never felt at ease long enough to have that. He'd lived with his guard up, his eyes always alert for that one person who might return for retribution.

"You want to see the lighthouse?" she asked.

"Does the coast guard give you access?"

"Sort of."

He cocked an eyebrow, intrigued and slightly amused.

She smiled, and they set off to tour the historic watchtower. They navigated their way through the back part of the house, occasionally brushing up against each other, exiting through a stubborn backdoor that had swollen from the weather. They admired the view of the gulf of Maine that led out to the North Atlantic Ocean. A short trip across the grounds led to the spectacular conical lighthouse. Instead of entering through the main door, Dana led him around the side to what appeared to be a storm cellar. Pulling keys from her pocket, she unlocked the deteriorating wooden doors and he helped swing them back. Small stone steps led down into darkness.

"Mind your step. Oh, and—" she was about to warn him, but it was too late. The steps were steep, but a beam of wood was a little too low for Jack's six-foot frame.

Jack rubbed his forehead. From therein he bent slightly at the hip and followed cautiously. A few seconds later, a light came on, revealing the stone coffin they'd entered. At least's that how it felt: claustrophobic and stuffy. The place smelt musty, like old clothes that had been left inside a closet for half a century. Dana shivered as a cool draft of air brushed against their skin. A few large beer barrels were stacked in the corner. The rest of the crumbling stonewalls were lined with wooden racks of dusty wine bottles.

"What is this place?"

"The safest place in Rockland Cove." She patted the face of a wall. "My father used to make his own beer and wine here. Before that, it offered protection from serious storms. Tornadoes and such."

The sound of wind picking up outside and an unknown object tumbling past the entrance way startled them.

"So no chance of this place collapsing in on us?" he said, observing again the dismal state of his surroundings.

"Not a chance. This place is built with rebar through the blocks and then covered in cement."

"For someone who runs a motel, you sure know a lot about construction."

She chuckled. "Numerous times growing up we had to dash in here when I was a kid—that was something our father always used to reassure us about. He said this place would be here long after us."

"Strong foundations," he muttered.

"Exactly. But it's what's underneath that matters."

"What?"

"That's what he'd say. Life would throw curveballs, and sometimes things around us collapse. Not much you can do about that. But it's what's underneath that determines if we can rebuild again."

Jack cast a glance around. "You had a smart father."

"Yeah. Yeah, I did."

In an unspoken agreement they continued on. On the far side of the room was another set of stairs that led to another door. After she'd unlocked it, they found themselves at the foot of a spiral staircase. Dana fished a flashlight out of her jacket and tapped it a few times on the palm of her hand. A beam of light flooded the floor.

"When the coast guard took over, they wanted the keys to the main entrance."

"You never gave them the keys?"

"We said they were lost."

"Were they?"

She jangled the keys and then led the way up the stairs.

"There are far too many memories inside of here. If they want to change the locks at some point, fine. But after they kicked up a fuss about us not letting them turn the house into a museum for public tours—"

"You said screw them."

"Something like that."

They chuckled, making their way up. The lighthouse was split into four rooms. The first floor was a storeroom with three loophole windows; the next held a kitchen, sink, fireplace, and a small amount of furniture; the third contained a bedroom with a curved cabin bunk bed custom-made to fit the shape of the room. The final was the lantern room with a small bench. They were unable to go up because it only offered the smallest amount of room.

"Hard to imagine that before the house was built, keepers used to live in here. Everything's been automated now. They installed a rotating aerodrome beacon back in '89. I wish they still had the old Fresnel one here; I would have loved to have shown you what my father used to do."

"They didn't change it until then?"

"He wouldn't let them." She glanced around her. "This is the oldest lighthouse in Maine. It's what made the place so appealing. My father didn't trust modern technology. That, and he was as stubborn as a mule. If he was still alive today," she pointed above, "this wouldn't be here."

"It must have been a lot of work."

"Without a doubt, but he loved it. Four times a night he would come out and wind the drum that made it rotate."

"Wind by hand, are you serious?"

"Yeah, the lens rotated using a weight, and that was driven by a clockwork mechanism."

He nodded slowly.

"I'm boring you. Sorry, a force of habit, I guess. So used to being around motel visitors who wanted to visit the lighthouse."

"You should be a tour guide."

She grimaced, and turned to leave.

"Guessing you don't have the same love for it as your father?"

"The place, yes," she hummed. "The work? No."

For a moment they basked in the silence. He noticed Dana stealing a glance at him from time to time. Beyond the small window they watched the light illuminate the treacherous waters and worn shoreline. Waves danced violently as a strong wind stirred up the ocean surface and battered the rocks. How many lives had been saved from the raging sea because of that light? How many more would? He snuck a glance at her sun kissed face. Shadows highlighted her features.

Despite his attraction, he had been trying all evening to resist the urge to reach for her. Was she waiting for him to make a move? He regretted feeling the need to pull away from her earlier in the evening, but it was for her own good. In as much as they had connected over the past week, Jack only had to think of his sister and why he was here to snap out of the fantasy. He couldn't allow himself to get close.

And yet, it was happening. There was a quiet magnetism between them, clearly evident by their body language and the way they continually locked eyes.

They retraced their steps and retreated to the house. The rain had begun to fall again, coming down even harder than earlier. The warm summer air had vanished in the blink of an eye only to be replaced by a sharp coastal wind that cut through them. It was almost a fight to close the door behind them. Water pooled around their shoes. In only a short distance the rain had drenched their clothes, leaving them chilled to the bone.

"Holy crap, where did summer go?" He shook out his hair.

"I told you it changes fast. I'll go grab some towels. I might even have one of Matt's old shirts."

"The towels are fine," he said.

The last thing he wanted was to make her feel awkward for the rest of the evening. Besides, wearing the shirt of the man he had attempted to kill? That wasn't happening.

Dana kicked off her flip-flops and padded cautiously away to avoid slipping. As she did, Jack noticed the way her dress clung to her curvy body, revealing her shapely ass, bra, and panties. She looked almost too good. He cursed Gafino's name under his breath and second-guessed his split second decision to pull away from her. A good woman was his weakness. Add to that someone who had shown him nothing but kindness since his arrival, and his ability to keep a level head was starting to crack. Then, of course, there was being holed up in a pen for the past four years with testosterone-fueled lunatics, sharing a cell with a guy who plastered the walls with pin-ups. That had only made his craving for the company of a woman once he got out that much stronger.

After all, he was only human. After their kiss, it was even harder to show restraint. It was brutal. He gave himself a mental shake, pushing the thought of seeing her naked from his mind. But as she returned, still dripping wet and carrying two soft white towels, the voice of reason became faint.

She handed him one. "Looks like we might be here for the night."

"The breakwater covers that quickly?" he said before wiping his face.

"It's not high. It's a little dangerous to try and head back, but we can if—"

"It's just one night, right?" he said, cutting her off.

She leaned her head to one side to dry her hair. "Yeah." She paused. "I just didn't want to make you feel any more uncomfortable than what I already have."

"You haven't."

Her eyes burned into his at his reply. The attraction between them was tangible. It was as if the very air itself had been statically charged, and Jack closed the distance between them. The sensible voice, the one that had told him to not get involved, was barely audible now.

Stepping into her space, she shifted from one foot to the other cautiously, before slowly lifting a hand, as if trying to gauge his intention or determine if she would just be rebuffed again. Finding him unflinching to her touch, she slid her hand around his neck to pull him in for a kiss. Without hesitation, his arm pulled at the small of her back, his mouth came down hard on hers with a fierce, hot kiss.

After a beat, they pulled apart.

"I was hoping you would do that," she said.

Lifting her off her feet, she wrapped her legs around him tightly. Cradling her in one strong arm while grasping at her hair with the other, his lips traced down her neck, licking and biting. Her skin was wet, cool to the touch, and tasted of summer rain. Stumbling back, he slammed into the wall before turning and supporting her weight against it. His hand slid up her skirt and around her ass. Her nails dug into the muscles of his back as though she was trying to rip his shirt apart. Hungry for each other and caught up in the moment, they didn't even register the frequent claps of thunder outside. Like unlocking a wild animal from inside its cage, their desire and primal instincts took over. Collapsing to the floor, they tore at each other's clothes. She tugged at his belt; he pulled at her panties until they were off. Their pulses raced faster.

She gasped into his mouth as their tongues encircled. Trembling and shivering in each other's arms, not even their excitement could warm them, still chilled by their soaked clothes.

He pulled back, breathing hard. "Shower. Where?"

Knowing what he had in mind, she gestured in the direction of a room further down the hall. He took her by the hand and led her down. Within a few minutes, steam filled every crevice of the large room, condensation fogging up the glass surrounding the shower. A trail of soggy clothes lay scattered and the blur of two bodies entwined reflected back in the mirror.

Even after they were done making love, a thin outline of a handprint remained against the glass; the fading evidence of wild, reckless, unruly passion.

23

LATER THAT EVENING, moonlight spilled into the bedroom through the skylight. The bed sheets shimmered as rain and silver light danced together on the pane of glass far above them. Dana rested her head on Jack's chest. Besides the sound of his heartbeat, the weather had eventually settled down and the house was silent.

"What about your parents?"

"They died when I was eighteen.

"So what happened?"

"I don't know the full details. A freak storm is what the coast guard called it. I was on the mainland at the time. Despite the lighthouse operating, they believe their boat smashed up against the rocks as they tried to steer it in." She paused as she reflected on the tragedy. "Ironic, isn't it? They had given their lives to protect others on this very ocean, only to end up suffering a fate that they had prevented so many others from having."

"I'm sorry."

"It's okay." She stroked the tips of her fingers across his body, exploring the ridges of his abs. "Some things, I guess, are just out of our control." She breathed in deeply as he caressed her arm.

"You miss them, don't you?"

"They…" She paused, contemplating what to say next before nodding slowly. "Yeah."

She lifted her head. "I still find it hard to comprehend the way your father and stepmother treated you," she said.

"He'd say it was the alcohol, but it was her. She egged him on."

"And what of your real mother?"

"Died in childbirth. At least, that's what I was told." He shook his head.

"You don't believe that?"

"It doesn't matter now; he got what was coming to him."

"What do you mean?

He met her gaze. "Ah, less about me."

She noticed the way he shifted the topic.

"You weren't speaking figuratively, were you?" he said, running his fingers across several scars she had on her chest and ribs. "How many times?"

"Four, five. Matt wasn't always like that. In fact, you

would have probably liked him in the early days. That is, when we first met."

"So why?"

"It was either Jason or me. I still, to this day, don't know what brought it on. But I know when it started. He used to do these trips into the city. Every time he came back, it was like living with a stranger. His nerves were on edge. He acted paranoid. He drank like a fish and, well, he denied it, but I found drug paraphernalia in his bag."

"Did you ever tell anyone?"

"I didn't need to. It's hard to keep secrets in this town, Jack. Gossip spreads like weeds if you don't collect your mail, or drop your kids off at school on a regular schedule. They call it the perks and woes of living in a small town."

When she dropped her chin, she felt his fingers lovingly trace her cheek. Her eyes lifted. A sympathetic half smile flashed on his lips before he gazed up at the skylight above them. She took his hand and kissed it. For the first time in years, she felt safe. There was no further exchange of words that evening. They both had shared an experience that no other human should ever go through. Secrets had scarred them physically and emotionally. His pain was hers, and likewise. Yet now that burden, and the guilt that she had carried for so long, no longer felt as heavy. His reaction wasn't full of self-righteous judgment, the kind that some folk in the town had been quick to dispense.

Why hadn't she reported it?

Why hadn't she left him?

She brought it upon herself, some said.

In Jack's arms, far from the past, the responsibilities of her daily life, and guilt, she was free. If only for that evening.

***

There was no telling when they fell asleep, only that when Jack awoke the sun was blazing. A deep orange light burned its way into the room, setting everything alight. They had slept in. The clock's red digits flashed almost ten. He cast a glance to Dana, who was still asleep beside him. Her figure intertwined with the white sheet that partly covered her naked body.

He watched her chest rise and fall for a while. Dry, and in the light of the morning, she was every bit as beautiful as the previous night. He knew he should have regretted his actions, notched it up to one too many drinks, but he didn't. He laid his arm across her and kissed her shoulder. She stirred a little, but didn't wake. Rising from the bed unclothed, he threw a towel around his waist and padded out. His head was throbbing from the alcohol. Shaking the fog from his mind, he searched the cupboards for coffee.

"Morning," a voice croaked.

He turned to find her wearing nothing more than a long blue jean shirt. It had to have been Matt's.

"Hey, I was just about to put a pot of coffee on. But I can't seem—"

She came up behind him, wrapping both arms around his waist and resting her head on his back.

"Second drawer on the right," she said before yawning.

Sure enough, that's where they were. He could have sworn he'd checked that drawer.

"Thanks." He turned into her, kissed her on the mouth gently, his mouth moving over hers ever so softly. Again he felt himself aroused by her touch, a pleasant reminder of an evening of passion. Behind them an intermittent buzzing sound made Dana pull away.

He couldn't resist watching her walk over to the table. She had a natural yet almost sultry sway to her hips and ass. The kind a man could get used to. As he lit the stove, Dana fished around inside her handbag for her phone. Just as he added a few scoops of coffee into the French press coffee pot, Dana let out a gasp.

"You're serious?"

He turned to find her face a picture of horror.

"I'll be right there."

"What's going on?"

"Jason's been arrested."

24

"DANA DROVE IN SILENCE, oblivious to the flurry of weekend traffic. Sunday afternoons were usually quiet in most towns. Rockland Cove wasn't like most towns. Vacationers clogged up the two lanes that weaved past stores. SUVs, motorcycles, and family minivans towing boats crawled forward bumper to bumper, some heading away from the marina, others returning to spend the day on the water. Jason sat in silence in the back while Jack rode shotgun. After several hours of waiting around to be seen while officers dealt with some pressing matter down at the harbor, Frank had finally brought them up to speed on what had happened.

It was early afternoon by the time they got out. Jason had been released on a conditional discharge with a court arraignment in a week.

Since leaving the police station, Dana hadn't said a word. It was her initial attempt at controlling the anger fuming beneath the surface, and partly not wishing to suffer any further embarrassment.

Shelly Evans, the mother of Jason's friend Luke, had already collected her son by the time they arrived. This was probably for the best, being as Dana assumed Luke was behind the whole incident and was prepared for a yelling match. Trouble seemed to follow that kid wherever he went; two suspensions from school in the past year alone, a marijuana possession charge that was dropped because he was a minor, and several incidents of destruction of property formed the basis of her quick judgment. If there was anyone who probably got a thrill out of fighting, it was him, she thought.

Surprisingly, though, that wasn't the case. No, according to Frank—who thankfully had been on patrol that night—Jason was adamant that Luke had tried to intervene. She was shocked, to say the least. Luke coming to his defense? An obvious cover story for his friend, but she'd know for sure soon. The police were going to gather a surveillance recording from Harley's, a local beer and liquor store whose cameras may have picked up the incident outside between Kyle and Jason. Frank had made it clear that regardless of whether or not Kyle was the instigator, he couldn't prevent his family from pressing charges, but he would give it his best effort to talk to them.

Brawls in Rockland Cove were a common occurrence. She wasn't sure if it was boredom, stupidity, or a combination of both. Either way, Frank had always made a point to keep most disputes between locals outside of the court system. Those he couldn't were usually handled pretty fast and severely. The very mention of court had her nerves on edge. He'd reassured Dana that he would put in a good word with Judge Mahoney, since it was Jason's first time being in trouble with the law. According to him, unless it was serious offense, minors were usually given a harsh warning, forced to apologize to the victim, performed a large number of hours of community service, and ordered to stay away from each other.

However that hadn't lessened her disappointment, anger, and utter disbelief over what he'd done. He'd put a kid in hospital, for God sake.

What had gotten into him?

She glanced in the rearview mirror for the thirteenth time, as if by some miracle she'd wake up from this nightmare and still find herself lying beside Jack.

"Aren't you going to say something?" Jason asked.

She flashed another look of disapproval, tapping a steady rhythm against the steering wheel while the truck jerked slowly forward behind the stream of traffic.

"What do you suggest, Jason?"

"I don't know? Chew me out. Do what you normally

do. Ground me."

"Ground you? You put a kid in hospital, Jason."

"I didn't start it. Kyle and his goons kicked off."

"Oh, so that gave you the right to finish it?"

"He's been on my case nonstop for the past year. What do you expect me to do, Mum? Keep taking a pounding every time?"

"No but—"

"There are no buts with Kyle, Mum. You are either a friend or a punching bag."

"Jason, his parents could press charges—never mind, send us the bill for his time in hospital. We can't afford that."

He scoffed. "They can."

"That's not the point."

"Mum, I barely scratched the guy."

"Oh, you call busting his eye up and knocking out three of his teeth barely scratching?" She paused to take a breath. "He could lose his eye—don't you get it? What the hell is wrong with you?"

He shrugged. "If people push, sometimes you've got to push back."

"That's the dumbest thing I've ever heard you say. Who told you that?"

Jack shuffled in his seat.

"Tell her what you told me, Jack."

Her eyes widened as she flashed Jack a look of disbelief. Jack dropped his chin and sucked air between his teeth. She couldn't believe it. Could this day get any worse?

The rest of the journey home was filled with awkward silence. For a moment she had thought things were beginning to look up. The evening with Jack had made her forget that all too familiar feeling of drowning. Slowly suffocating beneath a mountain of debt, a pile of accusations from town folk, and the adolescent woes of raising a teenage son. She had worked so hard to protect him from the backlash of Matt's disappearance. But there was only so much she could do. Had she known this was going to happen, she wouldn't have allowed him to sleep over at Luke's.

Heck, she wouldn't have even gone out. Now all she felt was regret about it all. She found herself wishing that she could have done something, anything, differently. Before Matt vanished and after.

Now there was Jack caught up in the middle of it all. A wild card she had never expected. She couldn't pretend that last night hadn't changed anything. It had.

And now this. She sighed.

***

By the time they had collected Apollo from the kennel and returned to the motel, dusk was setting in. While it was a gorgeous evening, none of them seemed to care. Dana was the first out of the truck. She didn't wait for either of them. Jason threw Jack a look that made it clear that he was sorry. Jack had him take Apollo for a walk while he went in to see if there was anything he could do to iron out matters.

Jack paused with his hand on the front door, contemplating his next move.

Inside, Dana was in the kitchen leaning against the sink. A soft breeze blew in from the open window. Her back was turned when he entered. He knew he was walking on eggshells, possibly about to speak where his opinion wasn't wanted, but this needed to be put into perspective. Maybe he'd become numb to years of violence, but a little rough behavior among teens wasn't anything to lose your cool over. The seriousness of it barely registered with him. In fact, unless there was mention of weapons involved or real threats of death, it was hard to take it seriously; but then again, he'd never had a kid.

"Dana. Look…"

Without turning she began, "Why would you say that to him? And what did he mean by, if it wasn't for you?"

Jack breathed out a heavy sigh. He wasn't prepared for this. Violent confrontations—those, he could handle. This was another reason he'd avoided getting involved with women beyond one night. They could never understand his line of work, his choices, his way of thinking, or how he dealt with situations. How could he ever have a normal conversation? To them, acts of violence weren't normal. To him, however, it was all he'd known.

"What I told him was my response to why I intervened with those bikers. I didn't think he would take it literally."

"You didn't think, that's right."

"And I may have shown him a few ways to protect himself."

"Protect himself?" She was beginning to repeat everything he said.

"If you weren't aware, Dana, he's been getting the shit kicked out of him by this kid on a daily basis."

"And you thought the solution was to show him how to do the same?"

"I thought he had a right to protect himself."

"Jack, that might work where you come from. But I'm trying to instill in my kid that fighting is not the answer."

"And what is? Taking a beating? There's no way in hell I would let my kid put up with that."

"You are not his father."

"No, I'm not, because if I was, I wouldn't have laid a hand on you."

"What? This has nothing to do with me."

"Oh c'mon, Dana, it has everything to do with you. If Matt hadn't laid a hand on you, do you think we would be having this discussion right now? You want to protect him from becoming like Matt. I get that. But you can't control your son forever. Give him some slack."

"You don't understand. Who the hell are you to tell me how to raise my son? If you hadn't taught him how to fight, maybe this wouldn't have happened. Have you considered that?"

"No, but then maybe it would have been your son in that hospital bed."

"Just go."

"Dana, I'm sorry."

"So am I. I think it's best you move out."

"Maybe it's best I just leave altogether."

She turned; her eyes met his before looking away. Gone was the loving gaze that she'd given him at the lighthouse. She didn't need to say any more; her eyes spoke volumes. That was all he needed to see to put this behind him. In many ways, the kid had done him a favor. He'd made it easier to leave. What the hell had he been thinking, getting involved with her? He would collect the money in the morning and be on his way.

Upstairs, he removed the few clothes she'd hung in the closet and stuffed them into his bag. He regretted how attached he'd become. It wasn't like him to get involved. It wasn't his way. And yet he had. For a moment, he thought he'd found someone who gave him a reason to change—a place where he could rest his head, and finish the remainder of his days away from the violence. A second chance to be something other than a killer. What a mistake that was.

His phone lay on the bed, buzzing. He ignored it.

No doubt it was Gafino. After Jack had phoned him from the café the previous night to let him know he'd found the money, he was probably calling back to confirm that all the loose ends had been tied up. Loose ends, of course, meant anyone who could tie him to the death of Dana and Jason. But they weren't going to die. He must have known that. He shook his head; if only he knew how deep he'd got. The entire town was a loose end. He'd played this wrong, that was for sure. No, he would tell Gafino it was done. Gafino had no reason to follow up. The only times he ever had was when he suffered a loss. As long as he had the stacks of green reflecting back in his eyes, a small town in the armpit of Maine would mean little to him. It was one more job completed. Rockland Cove would be nothing more than a distant memory that he'd soon forget.

They would go about their lives, and he'd be none the wiser.

25

DANA WATCHED JACK leave before stepping outside onto the back porch. She wondered if she was doing the right thing. Was he right? Would she have thought differently if it had been her son in hospital? If Matt had never beaten her black and blue, would she have had such aversion to violence? The thought of a court date on top of the past year, along with getting involved with someone she barely knew, only compounded the stress she felt. Even if he was what she wanted, it was the wrong timing. Maybe once she'd sold the motel, put a few more years between her and Matt; perhaps then she'd be ready for another relationship.

***

Jack heard him long before he saw him.

"Jack!" Jason shouted.

His cry broke through his mental focus. Jack had only made it down a few steps when Jason appeared out of the dark, his flashlight jerking all over the place. He turned toward the kid.

"I…"

"Slow down. Take a breath."

When he reached him Jason bent slightly, trying to catch a breath. His hands pressed against his knees as sweat dripped off his forehead.

"Apollo. I can't find him."

Jack's head turned from side to side. "What happened?"

"I…I was…I was with him out by the old barn. I tossed a stick; he shot off to get it but he never returned. I thought maybe he'd seen a rabbit or something. But he didn't respond to my call. I tried looking, but I don't where he is. I'm sorry, Jack."

Jack dropped his bag, rested his hand on Jason's back.

"Alright, it's okay; he's probably just being stubborn. Where were you?"

Jason pointed in the direction that he'd just come from. Jack took Jason's flashlight and headed out, calling for his dog.

The light from his flashlight skimmed the forest ground. The darkness beneath his light was alive. Unseen critters scurried beneath the cover of thick brush. It was pitch black. As the light fell upon a dark mound, Jack's eyes slowly grew wide, expecting the worst. Met with the horrific sight of Apollo's lifeless body, his stomach churned. He staggered back, unable to retract his gaze from the blood seeping out a gaping hole at the side of Apollo's head. A single bullet wound. Jason hadn't mentioned hearing a gunshot, and Jack himself hadn't heard a sound. A suppressor? He felt his skin come alive. Behind him, Dana and Jason caught up. He lifted a hand, trying to save them from the shock that had assaulted him.

"Get inside," he muttered, while his eyes whipped across the tree line.

The hair on the back of his neck lifted as he sensed someone.

"What? What the hell's going on, Jack?"

Jason stumbled forward, then gasped as he caught sight of Apollo. "Holy shit."

"Go. Now!" he yelled.

His voice carried for only a second before it was overridden by the snap of bullets. Turning on their heels in the direction they had come from, they raced toward the house, stumbling over fallen branches. Unable to pinpoint the spot the gunfire came from, Jack pulled his gun from his waist and backed up fast. Branches snapped beneath his feet.

Exposed. Out in the open. Surrounded by total darkness. All three were a lethal combination. He hadn't made it within five feet of the house when another hail of bullets snapped past him, shattering the windows of the sunroom. Jack moved from tree to tree until he was able to dash into the cover of the house. As he slid in across the floor, he could see Dana and Jason cowering beneath the table in the kitchen.

"Jack? Who's shooting? What the hell is going on?" Dana cried.

"I will tell you everything. Just stay put." He shot a glance out the window before scrambling over to them, keeping close to the ground.

"I'll call the police," she stammered, clinging to Jason.

"Don't," Jack said immediately.

He glanced at the cell in her hand. He let out a deep groan before passing Dana his Glock. "You know how to shoot one of these?"

"No."

"It's simple, just point and shoot. There is no safety."

The sound of a familiar taunting voice called out. "Come on, Jack. Don't make this hard."

He paused, throwing a cautious glance toward the back door before looking back at her and closing her fingers around the Glock 22. "Anyone comes in besides me, kill them. Don't think twice. Now, head upstairs."

"But I…"

"Just do it."

He watched as they hugged the floor in terror and disappeared into the hallway.

He scrambled over to the kitchen area. His eyes flicked across the counter. He yanked the drawer out, causing all the utensils to clatter onto the tiled floor. Scooping up the nearest items, a sharp knife and a bottle opener, he hurried down the corridor. Hunched over, he pulled back the blind covering the front door window. It was impossible to see if anyone was there. The house had no floodlights. It was a gamble either way he went. Front or back. No doubt they would have covered both. With his back pressed to the wall he waited in the darkness. In the silence he could hear his heartbeat.

"Jack. It's Freddy. We're not going to harm you."

The sound of Freddy's voice from outside was close. He couldn't have been more than a few yards from the front door. Jack hesitated before replying.

"He killed my dog, Freddy."

Keeping low, he moved tight against the floor. He knew never to stay in one spot.

"Fuck. Fuck it." He could hear the muffled sound of Freddy's voice just beyond the door.

Clearly Freddy had no idea. How many more of them were there? One out back, Freddy around front—had they brought others?

"Louis with you?"

"No, Jack. Just me and Tony. Come on out and let's talk."

This time his voice was closer; he must have been circling the house, since his position had changed. From this angle, crouched behind the sofa, he had a clear shot of the front door. He saw Freddy's silhouette through the glass. The door creaked open. The barrel of the gun appeared first, followed by the man himself. Jack tossed the bottle opener across the floor. It clattered and he rolled into position against the entrance wall. Holding his breath, he waited. Every fiber of his being was alert. The moment he saw Freddy's foot step inside, he jammed the knife down through his boot.

Freddy screamed in agony, letting off several rounds. Jack leapt up, grabbed his arm, and slammed his forehead into the man's face until he fell back to the floor, thrashing in excruciating pain. His foot was still stuck to the hardwood floor by the tip of the knife.

At the sound of the back door breaking off its hinges, Jack snatched the Beretta from Freddy, ran, and leapt out the open window.

Pulse racing, he knew he had a mere few seconds before Tony spotted him. Staying in the shadows, he circled around back. From inside, he could hear Tony yelling.

"Freddy? Where you at?"

The muffled cries of Freddy could be heard bouncing off the walls of the house. Jack heard a shotgun being pumped, and a shell hit the tiled floor. Like a piston he bolted up, stole a peek, and dropped back down. His breathing had become heavy. Inside, Tony cradled his weapon and prowled carefully through the kitchen area. Shattered glass crunched beneath his boots.

Jack crept forward with the Beretta lowered to the floor. As he flung open the door, everything started at once. Tony spun around, letting off several rounds that peppered the wall. Jack dropped to the ground, his arm slicing on glass as he pumped two shots into Tony, dropping him to the floor. Then there was silence, except for the groaning of both men. Jack rose to his feet, and without saying a word, he walked over to Tony. Still alive and coughing up blood, his former comrade's eyes grew wide. Without missing a beat, Jack unloaded three more rounds into his skull.

Lowering the gun, he walked to the hallway and returned to where Freddy was still writhing in pain. About to shoot him, Freddy threw up his hands.

"Jack. Jack, I swear. I was against this."

"Why, Freddy? Gafino knew I was going to bring the money."

"It was a setup, Jack. Gafino doesn't know."

Surprised and angered, he adjusted his grip on the

gun. "What?"

"Vincent. He's the one that orchestrated all of this. We were meant to collect the money, make sure the woman and kid were killed and then—"

"Kill me," Jack cut him off.

"No. Bring you in."

"Why?"

Through gritted teeth he spat, "Why do you think? Gafino. The old timers, they're things of the past. Vincent's calling the shots now. That whole drug deal— he was behind that. He had his own deal going. That's why it was never tested. You weren't meant to be there. But once Gafino got wind of it, well…"

Jack kept his gun locked on him.

"Think about it, Jack."

Jack recalled the day of the drug deal with Matt. Like a montage, the small overlooked things replayed in his mind. Matt had asked him, Where's Trig? Jack's mind flashed forward four years to the first time he saw Vincent. The tattoo on his knuckles spelled Trig. Nicky Civella had told Gafino that he'd given the money he owed to Vincent. Tony's words: You're not in charge, Vincent is.

"And Matt Grant?"

Freddy groaned in pain. "He's dead."

"So you take the money, bring me in to Vincent, and

then what?" Jack lifted his gun, keeping it fixed on him.

"Please, Jack." He groaned in agony.

"Tell me."

"He'd tell Gafino that you were gonna bolt with the money. That's all I know."

Jack nodded slowly. "So I'd be out of the picture, and no one would question him. But why wait to kill me?" Jack muttered to himself.

"He wanted you alive. Injured, but alive. What he had in mind from there he didn't say."

Freddy groaned while reaching for his foot.

"Give me your phone."

"What?"

"Your phone." Jack rifled through Freddy's pockets. Retrieving it, he brought up his contact list and pressed a number.

"Is it done?" Vincent's voice said on the other end a few seconds later.

Jack remained silent.

"Freddy?"

"He's unavailable," Jack replied.

There was silence on the other end.

"I'm coming for you," Jack said and then dropped the phone, crunching it beneath his boot and twisting his foot around.

Right at that moment, the faint sounds of cop sirens

could be heard in the distance. Barely able to form words because of the pain, Freddy pleaded for his life.

"Please, Jack, we've got history. I was just doing what I was told. You understand that, right?"

Jack stared at him for a moment before turning his head at the sound of a creak on the stairs. In that moment he saw a glint of silver out of the corner of his eye. Before Freddy could raise the gun he'd pulled from a holster around his ankle, Jack fired a round into his skull. His body went limp. A pool of dark blood spread out from his hair.

He stared at his lifeless body.

"You knew them?"

Startled, Jack twisted around to find Dana on the stairs. His own gun was aimed at him. Her face was a picture of pure horror. He took a step forward.

"Stay where you are."

"Dana."

He moved again, and as he did she haphazardly fired a round close to his feet, putting a hole the size of a dime in the flooring.

"Dana, this isn't what you think…"

Her eyes narrowed as if she was weighing his words. "You're here because of Matt, aren't you?"

He let out a sigh.

"Tell me!"

"Yes."

"Who are you?"

"I told you."

"Don't lie to me!" she screamed.

Her hands trembled as she tried to keep the gun steady. Jason slowly came down behind her. Both waited for an answer.

Jack nodded. "I work for the mob." He paused. "Well, I used to."

She grimaced. "A collector. Stupid. Oh my God, I can't believe how stupid I've been."

"Dana, let me explain."

Her hands were shaking. "Did you kill Matt?"

"No," he replied instantly, shaking his head. "God, no."

"Then why are you here?"

"It's complicated."

She shook her head in bewilderment. "And you weren't going to tell me?"

"There never seemed to be the right time."

"So are you going to kill us?"

"That's not what this is about."

"No?"

"I don't kill women or kids. Geesh, Dana, do you think I would have handed you my gun if I had planned on shooting you? If I wanted you dead, you already would be. You've got to believe me."

"How can I believe anything you've said or done?"

"I don't expect you to, but I would never harm you or your son."

The hands of time seemed to slow. Jack wasn't unaware of the two officers who'd entered through the door behind him, nor was he confused by their initial command to comply. He was very much aware of his world caving in. But it wasn't what would happen to him that bothered him the most. It was what could have happened to her—to them.

"Drop the gun, and get on the floor now," an officer repeated. "I won't tell you again."

He never took his eyes off Dana, even as he followed their orders and dropped to the ground. A firm knee bore down onto his shoulder, his hands locking behind his back. The sharpened teeth of handcuffs bit into his skin as they restrained him then hauled him out the door. His mind didn't register the words spilling from the roughneck cop's mouth as he read off the Miranda Rights. His thoughts were of her. Thrown into the back of a patrol car, he gazed toward the house. Sheriff Grant spoke briefly with her before returning to the cruiser. He was unable to make out what was said. The car spat up gravel as it swung a U-turn and headed out of the lot. Jack glanced back at Dana before the car rounded a corner. Jason stood in the cloud of exhaust as it drove away. Two officers remained on scene.

Seconds, maybe minutes, later an ambulance hurtled past them on their way to the station. A blur of lights painted the night sky as the siren became distant. Jack could see the officer's eyes shifting back and forth between the road ahead and the rearview mirror. Jack sifted through a barrage of thoughts. What had she told the sheriff? What would happen now? How would Vincent respond? He could feel his control of the situation slipping through his fingers.

26

TURNING OFF SUMMER STREET, the patrol car closed in on a medium, rectangular-shaped building with red brick. A short driveway led down to it from Portland Road.

It was vastly different from the busy police stations in the city. A few cruisers were parked out front. Unlike the city, where he was used to seeing cops trailing in and out at any time of the day, the exterior seemed more like a quiet library under the glow of lights.

Sheriff Grant and another officer dragged him out of the back and escorted him into the station. The inside had all the appearance of a museum. Old police artifacts and history were prominently displayed in glass cases, propped up on marble pillars. Brass plaques with the names of donators who supported a recent renovation filled another wall. On the station's main level was an area for fingerprinting and criminal record checks. Behind the usual bulletproof glass that surrounded the front desk were three desks. Various metal cabinets lined the walls; one contained rifles and shotguns, others were for files. There were only two other officers in sight. One was punching keys at a computer. He peered over his monitor briefly before resuming. The other was a staff sergeant who stood beside a bubbling percolator, pouring a cup of coffee.

"The shooter?"

"One of them," Sheriff Grant said, leading Jack into a booking area.

Handcuffed to the leg of a chair, Jack watched the officer rummage through a desk before tapping a few keys to bring up the details of the arrest that had been logged.

"Seems trouble has a way of following you, son." He tapped his pen on the table.

"I told you, it was self-defense. Dana will confirm it."

"Dana doesn't want you near her. She believes you are a danger."

Jack considered what he was saying while the sheriff glanced back at his screen and continued punching keys. Slowly, he leaned back in his chair.

"A stint in Rikers. Links to an organized crime syndicate. A criminal record a mile long." He paused. "Now I ask myself, what is someone with your background doing in our little town?"

"I told you."

"Right." He scoffed. "You're an antique collector."

"People have a right to a fresh slate, Sheriff."

"You know how many times I've heard that?"

Sheriff Grant looked at him for a moment, now tapping the end of his pencil in the palm of his hand. "So why the visit from these men? You owe them money?"

Jack stifled a laugh, dropping his head back.

"Something amusing?" The sheriff exchanged a glance with the staff sergeant before leaning forward and looking Jack in the face. "You are in a whole heap of trouble, son. I don't think you realize—"

"If you don't release me right now, you are going to have more blood on your hands."

The two officers regarded him, stone-faced.

"Then answer me. Who are the men, and why were they here?"

Jack remained silent.

The sheriff shook his head. "Get his prints. Put him in the holding cell."

"Am I being charged?"

"No."

"Then I'm free to go?"

"You are being held while we conduct our investigation."

The staff sergeant unlocked the handcuff and strong-armed him away.

"You're making a mistake, Sheriff."

The officer led him over to a fingerprinting area. Smearing his fingers in the pad of ink, he rolled each one on the paper until they had his ten digits. Jack didn't kick up a fuss. There was no point. He'd use what little time he had to think of what to do next.

Afterward he stood there while an officer rooted through his pockets, removed a few dollars in coins, a wallet, and his watch. His shoes were removed, since obviously they didn't want him hanging himself with shoelaces. Jack shook his head in amazement. He placed all his belongings in a tray. Later it would be bagged and tagged.

From there the cop led him over to an adjoining area. The cell block was on the same floor. No need to climb stairs or go down elevators. It gave them easy access. Divided into five cells, on the outside they looked like any typical rooms, except for five large metal doors. All of them were made of dull industrial steel, built to withstand any fits or drunken outbursts.

Inside there was a place to piss, a steel water fountain, and a bench that was an extension of the wall itself. Cinder blocks for walls were covered in thick cream paint. A large number three was painted in red on the wall, indicating which cell it was. By all accounts it was plush compared to Rikers, but it was still your typical cell. As the cell door clanged behind him, he felt his stomach turn at the sound of the key in the lock. He'd imagined he would never hear another cell door close. How foolish that had been. Jack wandered around the cramped cell in circles, staring at the walls. Taking off his jacket, he slung it down onto the bench and took a seat.

Charged or not, he didn't like being held one bit. Out of sight, out of mind had always been his policy. He reassured himself that all they had was circumstantial evidence. There was no way they could know why he was there, unless Dana had told them. But she couldn't have; otherwise, they wouldn't have been asking what his connection to the men was. Why hadn't she told them? What had she said to the sheriff? Better question: What had her husband told her before he was killed? Logic said she didn't know about the money, but maybe Matt had told her not to touch it. He laid there, his mind in turmoil, tossing around questions. Beyond the door, muffled police communication transmitted over the radio. A phone rang. Footsteps passed his door, and the noise of computer keys being punched blended together.

It wouldn't be long before they figured out who the men were. Before they located Matt's bones, wherever they had dumped him. And yet that wasn't what concerned him most.

Vincent wouldn't wait for him to show up; he would strike first.

That's what Jack would have done. He had to get out. Speak to Dana. Get her and Jason to safety and finish this. But how? He pressed fingers against his forehead and began kneading to relieve the band of pressure building. Minutes, then hours, passed. Pent up energy eventually turned into exhaustion and his eyes closed.

***

When his crusted eyes blinked open, he noticed his jacket was damp with drool. With the zipper squished into the side of his cheek, he let out a groan, turned over, and glanced at his wrist. They had confiscated his watch along with all other personal items. The events of the evening played out again. Sadness overwhelmed him at the thought of Apollo. He shook his head around, clearing the fog from his mind. There was no way of telling how long he'd been asleep or how many hours had elapsed. He rose to his feet and stretched out his aching joints with a grunt. The muscles in his back ached. Rubbing the back of his head, he leaned against the cell door and banged on it.

"Hey!" he yelled as he continued slamming the door with a closed fist.

Several minutes passed before an officer appeared through the slot in the door. Jack immediately recognized him as one of the officers who had remained on scene at the motel.

"You want to stop banging on the door?"

"What's the time?"

"Close to seven."

He'd slept the night away. A wave of anxiety crashed down on him.

"Don't I get a phone call?" he replied.

"You haven't been charged."

"I still want my phone call."

The officer scowled at him. "Hang tight."

He slammed the metal shutter on the door. Jack ran a hand through his hair. It wasn't long before his mind started thinking the worst. A short time later, he heard the noise of heavy boots approaching. The lock turned, and Sheriff Grant swung the door open.

"Let's go." He made a gesture with a wave of his arm.

"Where you taking me?"

"County." He paused as Jack threw him a confused glance. "The county sheriff's office is in Sanford. This is just a satellite office."

Jack rolled his eyes as he slipped his coat back on, and approached the door.

"I thought I wasn't being charged."

"As it stands, you're not. But I have two dead bodies on my hands."

"And I told you—" Jack said.

"Self-defense. Right. But there is still procedure we have to go through. You'll get a chance to tell your side of the story to the judge."

As he stepped out, the sheriff slapped a pair of handcuffs on him.

"Are these really necessary?"

"Precaution. I'm sure you understand."

Jack shook his head. "You think I'm a threat?"

"I think there are things you are not telling me."

27

IN THE CRUISER, neither Jack nor Frank spoke until they were on the highway. Jack occasionally saw Frank's eyes glance at him in the rearview mirror. Years gone by, Frank would have been dead by now. Life in Gafino's world had taught him that it was better to kill than to be taken in. No one trusted anyone. Most would give up their own mother if it meant getting a lower sentence. They all knew that. That's why it hadn't surprised him when there were multiple attempts on his life inside. It was also the reason they had never visited him in four years. Out of sight, out of mind. It was a motto they were taught to live by.

Jack had never murdered a cop, but there had been times he'd come close to it. Fortunately, he'd escaped custody many times. Chased through the subways, across rooftops, and busy streets. It was a game that had excited him when he was a teen. The thrill of being chased or pursuing another made him feel alive, whether that was a cop or a gang member. It didn't matter.

Jack squinted as the light momentarily blinded his eyes. The yellow sun was beginning to rise above the tree line, feeding the air with humidity and heat. No doubt it would again be a hot day. Few cars passed them on the way out of town.

His mind drifted back to a time when wrongdoing felt right and anything but his life seemed absurd. In the early hours, a favorite pastime of his was drinking coffee at one of the many cafés in the city and watching the masses on their way to their menial, soul-crushing jobs. How many of them rose each day and were truly happy about their life? Slaves to a corporate world, an existence they only wished was as exciting and dangerous as the one he led. How many of them spent a few hours each evening escaping their lives of desperation immersed in tales that were based on a life he actually lived? Contract killer, assassin, a gun for hire. Only glamorous portrayals that most assumed were nothing but tales were very real and far from glamorous.

He would have traded it all to live a normal life. Getting the job done without any emotion is what had earned him his reputation. Where others trembled, faltered, and collapsed under pressure, Jack rose, only becoming more confident with each passing year. Yet for all the confidence he had, it was nothing more than a false sense of security. He wasn't immortal. He couldn't outrun trouble for long. Eventually even those who had revered him changed their tune and hated him. Jealousy burned strong among crime families. Everyone wanted to be a made man, a somebody in an ocean of faces. They would think nothing of clawing their way to the top, even if it meant stepping on toes, crushing fingers, or stabbing another in the back. Of course, on the surface, those around him held their cards close to the chests. That was what separated those who won from those who lost. It was all a game. No, what he came to learn was those who were taken into the inner circle weren't feared or revered; they were loathed.

"Taking a different route?" Jack asked, noting they had missed the exit sign for Sandford.

"I need to swing by Dana's. Pick up her written statement," Frank responded.

Jack's brow knit together. "Wouldn't the officer last night have taken it?"

"If she was in the right frame of mind. But after what she went through...There was no rush."

"Yeah, I noticed that. Must be a small town thing."

Frank lifted his eyes to the rearview mirror. "And by that you mean?"

"You know. After the biker incident, I would have

imagined a background check would have given you ample reason to question my motives."

"Why? Are you trying to hide something?"

"I have nothing to hide."

"Right. That's why you were so forthcoming about who those men were."

Jack's mind churned over details from the previous night. Something had been niggling at him, something didn't quite add up. As they pulled into the parking lot outside the motel, the sheriff killed the engine.

"I'll be right back."

Before he exited the vehicle, Jack spoke. "Tell me, Sheriff. When you showed up last night, how did you know?"

"What?"

"How did you know about the men being there?"

"A neighbor reported gunshots."

Jack locked eyes with him. The sheriff flashed him a look that made him feel uneasy. Slamming the door on the car, he watched Frank make his way up the steps to the house. Jack pondered what he'd said. He recalled what Jason had said the day they fired off some rounds.

They've never called the cops.

Jack noticed four things. Behind the office window was the "WE'RE NOT OPEN" sign. The power to the main sign had been shut off. Dana's Ford truck was gone, and in its place was a black sedan. His pulse began to race. Jack strained his neck to see the back of it.

It had a yellow New Jersey license plate.

Realizing the precarious nature of his position, his eyes flicked back to see Frank standing at the door. He was speaking with someone, but he couldn't see who it was.

Jack had to act fast.

He slipped the cuffs from behind his back under his legs. Diving between the two seats until he could get in the driver's side, he went for the keys—but they weren't there.

Operating on pure instinct, he tore at the plastic panel beneath the steering column. His heart thumped hard in his chest. Once the ignition cylinder was visible, he yanked free a collection of colored wires leading to it. To any other person it would have been confusing, but to him it was like tying shoelaces. It didn't matter what car it was; they all functioned the same. Two red wires handled the power, and two brown wires were connected to the starter. After the longest minute of his life and few hot sparks, the car rumbled to life.

"Hey," the faint sound of the sheriff's voice coupled with the sight of Louis storming out of the house sent his mind into overdrive.

Still handcuffed, he slammed the car into reverse with both hands, tearing backward at breakneck speed. He spun the car a sharp one-eighty, almost losing control. Two shots rang out, and the back window shattered. Shards of glass covered the backseat. The tires barely gripped the tarmac as Jack hammered the accelerator to the floor and the car surged out, spitting up gravel. If there had been an easy way out of this tangled mess before, it was all but gone now.

***

"What the hell are you doing?" Vincent lowered Louis' arm as he charged past him. "I want him alive, you idiot."

"You really think he's going to tell you where the money is?"

"The money's the least of my concerns."

As they hopped into the black sedan, the sheriff joined them. His face was sweating and red, as if he'd had one too many whiskeys. "You swore this would be contained."

"Well, had you brought him up to the door or kept the bitch at the house, we wouldn't be in this position, now would we?"

"This has gone too far."

Vincent sneered as he pointed his gun at the sheriff. "Sheriff, you wanna join your son? No? Then your better keep your mouth shut, and do as I tell you."

Beside him, one of Vincent's men flashed Grant a grin while pulling out his own handgun. Frank's eyes darted between them. Vincent turned his head back toward the road as Louis floored it.

28

JACK SQUEEZED THE WHEEL tight as the cruiser roared its way beyond the town, tires squealing and pushing the engine to its limits. His eyes darted back and forth between the rearview mirror and the road ahead. Every nerve was on high alert. Only one thing now shot through his mind: Getting to Dana and Jason before Vincent. A green sign for Rockland Breakwater Lighthouse, indicating five miles, flashed past in his peripheral vision. There was one road in, one road out. Where else could they have gone? It was the only place she felt safe. They had to be there. The sound of the police radio to his right brought home a harsh realization. He'd stolen a police car, and his word against an officer of the law wouldn't stand up. Jack hammered the wheel with a balled fist as he tried to comprehend the sheriff's involvement.

Then, from seemingly out of nowhere, the black sedan

appeared behind him, speeding up and closing the gap between them. Jack instantly went into diversionary tactics, skating the shoulder and fishtailing the width of the road to prevent them from coming up alongside him. He pinned the gas and maneuvered the cruiser with fearless confidence despite still being cuffed. With the back window shot out, he expected nothing less than more brutal violence. Sure enough, he heard the snapping of bullets. They were trying to take out a tire.

Rumbling down the open road, he pushed the car to a speed of almost hundred and twenty. His eyes were on fire, alert to every attempt to come up beside him. Jack knew if he didn't stop them before he reached the breakwater, he would have little chance.

Jerking the wheel to the left, he released pressure off the accelerator and allowed them to slide up, catching a glimpse of Vincent for a split second. Before they were completely parallel, he slammed the brakes to the metal and slid behind them almost effortlessly. Smoke billowed up off the tires as he pinned the gas, and hightailed it up behind them. A foot, then inches from the bumper, he plowed hard into the back of the sedan. The vehicle's tires screeched as they tried to keep control. Again he forced the cruiser directly into their rear. Both headlights' glass shattered, and the bumper tore away. Barely hanging by a thread of metal, it scraped the asphalt, kicking up hot orange sparks. Each time he slammed into the back he saw them jerk forward. Relentless, he didn't let up for a second.

As if anticipating the next assault, Vincent tried to keep him from coming up alongside them. With each hit, Jack's ability to keep control was getting harder.

Then he saw his opening.

Jack hammered it, adrenaline surging through his tense body. The front end slid up the right side. Aligned to the back wheels of the sedan, he braced himself. Within a fraction of a second, too fast for them to counteract, he executed a dirty but effective PIT maneuver and rammed the corner of the patrol car just behind their back wheel. Metal crunched and hot sparks spat wildly before the sedan abruptly turned sideways.

Jack slammed his brakes.

Unable to keep control or stop, the sedan launched off the hard shoulder and landed with a sickening thud. Soil kicked in the air; small trees and undergrowth flattened as it continued down the embankment and collided with a thick tree stump.

The car idled as he waited a minute or two to observe the aftermath.

Black smoke rose from the crumpled front end. Instinct told him to get out and make sure they were all dead, but the risk was too high. Injured or not, going up against them handcuffed and with no weapon would be foolish. Then there was that little matter of the cops. Police could be on scene any moment. Who knew if the sheriff had called them in? He cranked up the radio inside the car. It crackled. A couple of officers mumbled about an incident on the west side of town. A domestic between a couple they had dealt with before. He cast a glance back to the sedan. Flames now engulfed the engine. Still listening to the radio system, he didn't hear mention of his escape, which only confirmed his earlier suspicions about Sheriff Grant.

Jack took one last look, only to see Vincent's bloodied frame drop out of the driver's side window and collapse. He didn't wait around to see the other three crawl to safety. A spiral of gray and black smoke appeared in his rearview mirror as he peeled away.

***

Dana could barely concentrate on her drive out to the lighthouse. Something about it all just didn't add up. Churning it over, her stomach felt queasy, and not even the sight of her parents' home made her feel safe. But staying at the motel wasn't an option. The department didn't have the manpower to leave an officer on scene; at least, that's what she was told, and the whole incident had scared her on so many levels. She was still in shock. Her mind was a nonstop highway of questions, each one crowding out all sense of normalcy.

Had Jack been telling the truth? Who had killed Matt? And if Jack had been sent by the mob, why hadn't he killed her?

He'd had plenty of opportunity.

But maybe she was looking at this from the wrong angle.

Having been married to Matt for twelve years, she had thought she knew him. Sure, their financial difficulties were a burden that came between them, but still, what on earth would have got into him to get wrapped up with the mob? And over what? An unpaid loan? Drug money? If there was any, she hadn't seen it.

She searched for answers in her memories. Any sign, indication, phone call that she'd overlooked. All she had to do was close her eyes and Matt was there. Their arguments replayed in her head. The nights when he would return from the city were always the most brutal. The heated shouting matches over how they were going to pay the bills and her failed attempts at trying to discuss the sale of the motel had always been a sore point. In his mind, to sell the property was to declare himself a failure. To her it was just common sense. In the final year before his disappearance, she had avoided any subject that didn't involve bringing him his supper or Jason needing picking up. The beatings had become more frequent and always followed his returns from the city. It had reached a boiling point and forced her to sleep in a separate bedroom. She knew it was only a matter of time before they divorced or she wound up hospitalized.

They had lived on borrowed time—that was for sure.

Then, as she sifted through his words and actions, she remembered one thing he'd repeated in a drunken state before his final trip into the city. He'd been slouched in his La-Z-Boy armchair, surrounded by four empty bottles and the scraps left over from his meal.

"Tomorrow it's all gonna change," he'd muttered.

Those had been his last words. Slurred, almost incomprehensible—they made as much sense now as they had then, but then again she'd gotten used to ignoring anything that came out of his mouth. Promises, threats, and pleas for forgiveness were usually what spilled from it. In many ways, he had become a shadow of his former self.

Nursing a cup of coffee, she heard the faint spitting sound of gravel outside. It was rare to hear anyone approach the house; it was common knowledge in the town that it was private property. The only ones who came out were utility workers and the coastguard.

"Who is it, Jason?" she said, taking a sip of her coffee.

Hauling himself off the couch, he kept his eyes on the baseball game on the TV.

"Well?"

He cast a glance outside before returning to his seat. "It's the police."

She frowned. She had already given a statement. Not that she had given them much. She wasn't sure why they would come all the way out here when a phone call would have sufficed. Perhaps they had extracted more from Jack? Maybe they had more on him? Or she'd forgotten to sign the paper?

When she reached the screen door, her eyes widened. She blinked. The mug slipped from her hand, and coffee splashed all over the pine floor. At the clatter of ceramic breaking, Jason bolted up from the couch.

"Mum?"

"Get upstairs."

With desperation and purpose, Dana didn't think twice. Racing over to the double-barreled shotgun above the fireplace, she wrenched it off the wall hooks, feeling its weight in her hands. Cradling it in one arm, she snapped it apart and reached for a box of shells in a nearby drawer. All the while she kept her eyes on Jack, who was approaching the house at a fair clip.

The cartridges scattered as she emptied the box from the side. Some rolled off the side of the table and clattered on the floor. Punching two cartridges into the chamber and locking it in place, she turned around just in time to find Jack stumbling into the hallway.

She raised the gun and yelled, "Don't come a step closer!"

Jack was panting hard. He held up his handcuffed hands, speaking slowly. "Listen to me, Dana. Put the gun down." He cast a glance back over his shoulder. "I'm not here to harm you. But there are men coming who are."

She glanced back out the window toward the cruiser. "How did you get out? Where's Frank?"

"He's a part of this."

"A part of what?"

Jack cast a cautious glance outside. "Listen; there is no time to explain."

"You've got two minutes to tell me what's going on, or as God as my judge, I will shoot you where you stand."

He smirked ever so slightly. "Dana, I've seen how you shoot."

She squinted. "Not with a shotgun you haven't."

He let out an exasperated sigh. "Fine, but get these off me."

He motioned with the cuffs.

"They stay right where they are. Now start speaking."

She kept the barrel leveled at his chest as he began to bring her up to speed: his first time meeting Matt, his time inside Rikers, and his sister being used as leverage to force him to take on one last job. How he'd imagined it would be a simple collection: in and out. He'd never intended anyone to get hurt.

"A little late for that, don't you think?"

He could see the pain in her eyes. She had already suffered more than anyone should have.

"I know I've not given you any reason to trust me. And I'm not looking for forgiveness for my past. I'm trying to do what's right here."

"Which is?"

"Keeping you and Jason safe."

"Why?"

Before he could reply, his eyes picked up a dark moving dot in the distance, making its way up the breakwater. Trailing behind it was a plume of dust, spurring speed and the urgency for him to act.

"They're coming."

She glanced out.

"You need to decide right now who you'll trust. If not for your own sake, do it for Jason."

He stepped closer, holding his cuffs down and pulling them apart. "Shoot."

She hesitated, a look of anger spreading across her face. Jack turned his head.

"Shoot them, now!" he yelled.

Aiming at the cuffs, the tip of the barrel touching the metal chain, she pulled the trigger. A sudden explosion, a ringing in his ears, then he was free.

"You're going to need this."

Jack turned to see Jason holding his Glock. Jack squeezed his shoulder before taking it and tucking it behind the small of his back. He reached for the shotgun in Dana's hands. Reluctantly she released her grip, allowing him to take it.

"Do you have any other guns?"

"In the gun cabinet."

Jason ran to retrieve one.

Jack gave another quick look over his shoulder. "Is there any other way off this place?" he asked.

"Um. Yeah," she said nervously. "There's a small boat my father used for fishing."

"Go. Go now. Don't look back. No matter what you hear."

Snatching what cartridges he could and tossing them into his pockets, he gave them one final glance as they raced out the back.

Jack's heartbeat was a drumroll as he headed for the front door. Not missing a beat, he quickened his pace and ran toward the cruiser. Dropping down behind it and panting hard, he closed his eyes. Taking a deep breath, he willed his pulse to slow. There had been numerous times in his life where he'd had to confront armed thugs; however, he'd always had the element of surprise. He had known who he was up against, and by the time they could react he had dropped them.

But this, this was different. He knew very little about Vincent, other than the fact that he was younger than him. He wasn't invincible; the years had slowed him and time inside made him feel rusty. He snuck a peek around the corner of the bumper.

The dot in the distance was now clearly defined. A blue V8 Ram truck roared its way toward him. He wondered if the occupant had been killed. He knew there was no other way he could have gotten a vehicle in such a short time.

He waited until they were within seventy-five yards, give or take, before he was sure it was Vincent. Convinced, he hauled himself up and strode forward without fear. He knew the moment they reached the house his chances of being hit were high. Stopping them was unrealistic, but to inflict as much damage before they got close, that was doable. He unloaded a round into the engine. Steam burst out. Pinning the gas, it began picking up speed. With an arm out the window and the sun reflecting off the steel of a gun, Louis returned fire. Jack focused, and with his breath under control, he pulled back the trigger a second time. A round slammed into the window.

Breaking open the shotgun, Jack pushed in more slugs and retreated back to the house, firing off one more defensive round. As he dove into the house, the truck collided with the cruiser, cutting the power to the engine. Vincent immediately leapt out and took cover. Crouching down, he unleashed a series of shots at the house. Glass shattered all around. Tunnels of light permeated the house. Jack returned fire using his Glock before quickly reloading the shotgun. As he snuck another glance out the window, he saw Louis had slipped out and taken cover behind the tail end of the cruiser. He was still alive, but clutching a bloodied shoulder. Behind him the sheriff moved into position, along with Mickey Dunn. Dunn had been working for Gafino for as long as he could recall. He was a huge black guy who spent more time pumping himself with steroids and lifting steel than doing any work. There wasn't a time his clothes didn't look as if they were bursting at the seams.

"Just give them the money, Jack," the sheriff hollered.

"I would, but this isn't about money, is it, Vincent?"

Jack watched as Vincent motioned with two fingers to Louis to circle the house while Dunn went the other way. Jack punched out the window with the end of the barrel and fired a round off, sending the sheriff scrambling for cover. Among the sound of bullets pinging off metal and the sheriff and Vincent returning fire, he was distracted from the threat that bore down on him from the rear.

"Son, you're making a big mistake!" Frank shouted.

Jack clenched his jaw; every tendon tensed as his eyes flicked back and forth from the front to the rear of the house. For a split moment, he thought he caught sight of Dunn pass the window. He knew he had possibly only ten, or fifteen, seconds before they would be in the back door. Keeping low to the floor, Jack scrambled to the other side of the room. All the while he could hear the sound of Frank outside, trying to negotiate him out. The guy was a fool. He'd be dead the moment he stopped being useful.

The next sound was the back door creaking. The sound of boots on the wood floor was hard to mask. The two of them were inside. Jack pressed close to the wall and listened. Jack caught a glimpse of Dunn in the glass, moving down the hallway. Closing his eyes for just a second, he swung his gun out and blasted two shots while moving out of the line of sight. Dunn jumped out of the way, crashing into another room. Louis wasn't even in the hall. Jack replayed the layout of the house in his head before hearing the floor creak again. This time, several shots rang out through the drywall close to Jack's head. Dust and drywall filled the air. Crouching down, Jack headed for the next room.

What happened next occurred fast. Jack could hear Dunn coming closer from behind the wall. He stepped back and emptied his gun through the barrier. For a second he thought Dunn was returning fire, but it was Louis. The man was on him faster than he could react. One of the bullets hit him in the arm. As he swung around to defend himself, Louis drove the butt of his shotgun square into his face. Jack dropped to the floor, hard.

Before he lost consciousness, he saw the silhouette of Vincent entering through the front door.

"The girl?"

Lois shrugged.

"I'll get her," Frank said. Jack's eyelids blinked rapidly as he slipped in and out of consciousness. The next moment he opened them, Vincent was kneeling down close to him, grinning.

"One man. That's all you could take down? You're getting slow, Jacky boy."

The next thing he felt was Vincent's fist, then everything went dark.

29

"DANA, WAIT!" Frank cried out.

By the time he'd reached them, they had carried a small fishing boat down to the water. Jason was sliding it in while Dana looked on.

"It's all over. It's okay." He waved his arms frantically. Dana cupped her hand to shield her eyes, muttered something to Jason and then walked toward him. Once she was within a close proximity, he tried to explain that Jack had escaped, but that he was secured now.

He could see hesitancy in her face. She looked past him then back at him.

"Where's Jack?"

"In the back of a cruiser. It's okay, you're safe."

He stepped forward.

"I don't believe you."

He was about to lunge at her when she raised the rifle.

***

"You don't remember me, do you?" Vincent scoffed. "But then again, why should you? The butcher doesn't kill children."

"You've lost me."

"Allow me to refresh your memory."

Vincent reached into his jacket pocket and tossed what looked like a folded piece of card at him, dog-eared and crinkled. Jack could see it was a Polaroid. He took it between his bloodied fingers.

"Remember him?"

Jack stared blankly at the aged photo.

"You should. He was your first kill."

Jack's fingers smeared the image in blood.

"My father—or, as you remember him, Jimmy Burke."

It had been many years since he'd seen that face. The events of that day played in his head. The look of surprise on Burke's face as he touched the wound, as blood poured from it. As Jack turned to leave, he noticed a young boy peering out the back window of Burke's car. There was something about the way he had stared at him that had never left his mind.

Jack coughed. Blood trickled from the side of his mouth.

"I was a very different man back then."

Vincent smirked. "The Butcher grew a conscience."

***

Dana shifted back, re-adjusting her grip on the pump action rifle pointed at Frank.

"Dana. You don't want to do this. I can help."

"Like the way you helped Matt?"

"I don't know what Jack told you, but it's all lies."

"You said you didn't see Matt that night."

"I don't know what you're—"

"Don't you dare tell me you don't know what I'm talking about! You allowed people to believe I might be responsible. You used me."

"I never intended—"

"Save it for someone who cares, Frank. All I want to know is what happened that night."

"I don't know."

"Bullshit. I swear, you tell me one more lie…"

She worked the action to chamber a round. He raised his hand in defense. "Wait. Why do you care?"

"He was still Jason's father," she said slowly.

"But we both know what he was doing to you."

"Yeah, and you did nothing."

Frank took off his hat and rubbed his brow with his forearm. The heat of the noon sun bore down on them intensely. His eyes dropped to the ground before staring off to the house.

"He was stubborn. You know that."

"Bullshit. You were more concerned about how it would affect your career, your reputation. The way people would shun you. A sheriff's son…"

He looked up. "Dana, you know how long I've been doing this job? Do you know what it took to get where I am? I tried, I really did. He refused help. I tried to reason with him, but he wouldn't listen."

"And that night?"

He shook his head, a look of exasperation or guilt spreading across his face. "If he'd just given them the money, maybe…" He ran a hand around the back of his neck.

"So, what, you killed him?"

"I didn't kill him." He paused and his chin dropped. "They did."

"And you stood by and did nothing?"

He was silent, as if the weight of remorse was more than he could bear.

"You just turned a blind eye?"

"You don't understand, Dana, I tried. I tried to help him. But he signed his own death warrant the moment he went down the path of drugs. If they didn't kill him, the drugs would have. You should know better than anyone how many times I came rushing to his aid. How many times I risked my reputation, nearly lost my career, over his blatant disregard and irresponsibility. I warned him that the next time I wouldn't get involved. These men don't mess around."

She grimaced. "But you were his father?"

Frank's eyes dropped.

"What happened to you, Frank?"

"This career is what happened. It's taken everything: my wife, my kid. You know, I had high hopes for that kid of mine? Did he ever tell you how I wanted him to join the department? You know, follow in my footsteps?" He sucked at his teeth, looking out over the water. "That wasn't going to happen. It just wasn't in the cards."

He pressed the tips of his fingers against his forehead.

"No one wants their child to go off the rails, Dana. But we can't control their decisions forever or the people they run with."

She studied him. "But you swore an oath to protect."

"Don't you think I know that? I have to live with this every day." He shook his head. "I hate the reflection in the mirror." He groaned. "Every day. Every damn day, I put a gun to my head thinking this is going to be it. The day I end it. But I can't even do that. Because I'm a coward, an old fool." He paused. "Dana, I didn't have a choice. They would have killed both of us."

"We always have a choice," she replied.

He looked at her, then turned his attention to Jason, who appeared equally stunned by Frank's admission.

"Leave now. Go. I will tell them you were gone. Just go."

Dana slowly took a step back with Jason closely behind. They were about to make their way down the dock to the boat when Jason was thrown to the ground. Dana spun around to feel the harsh back slap of Louis' hand on her face. The rifle dropped to the dock then bounced into the water. As it disappeared below its murky surface, her heart sunk. She reached for her cheek, feeling the sting. It burned.

"What the hell are you doing?" Louis shouted at Frank.

Frank raised his hand slowly toward his sidearm.

"Just hold—"

Before he could react, Louis fired a round at Frank, hitting him in the neck. He crumpled to the ground.

"Damn pigs, can never be trusted."

Writhing in the dirt, only the sickening sound of Frank choking on his blood could be heard, mixed with the waves lapping against the shore. Louis set off in the direction of where he lay, assumedly to finish him off.

Dana knew it was now or never. She had no doubt. They had mere seconds to react before he turned the gun on them. Making a mad dash for the boat wasn't an option. She grit her teeth, grabbed her son's arm, and sprinted for the lighthouse.

So petrified at the thought of dying they didn't look back to see if he was hot on their heels. Sweat poured between her shoulder blades. They hadn't made it more than ten yards from the storm cellar when a gun went off. The sound of the bullet was horrifying enough, but when it ricocheted off a nearby metal surface making it clear it was intended for them—fear took over. Dana stumbled to the ground, physically and emotionally drained. Jason clasped her hand to draw her up, but she couldn't move. Like a blast of cold liquid nitrogen, she froze. All she could do was wait for the inevitable next bullet.

Then it happened. A short, sharp crack.

30

VINCENT CIRCLED JACK like a rabid animal, never taking his pistol off him for a second. Jack blinked hard and wiped at the corner of his right eye, a trickle of blood from his head blurring his vision.

"You waited this long to seek retribution for your father's death? Why didn't you just kill me when I was on the inside?"

"Ah, Jack, you're not seeing the big picture here. You might have pulled the trigger, but Gafino ordered the hit. These things take time. You should know that."

"So what, you're going to kill Gafino? You don't think he has a contingency plan in place in the event of his death?" Jack muttered, spitting out another glob of crimson red. "You'll be dead before you get out of New Jersey."

Vincent laughed. "Who said I was going to kill Gafino? A lot's changed since you were out, Jack. Gafino is hanging by a thread. His reputation is shot. His whole operation is a stack of cards waiting to collapse. People don't trust or respect him like they used to. They want fresh blood, not these old timers. Why do you think Freddy, Louis, and others got on board?"

Jack spat blood on the ground and chuckled.

"You came to destroy what you despised only to become what you despised."

"What can I say? The money is good."

"You gonna kill me or what?"

"I don't want to kill you, Jack. Well… not yet. But I'll tell you what I do want. I want you to suffer. To feel pain. To know what it's like to have your life torn from you. I want to see it in your eyes. So I'm going let you watch as I tear apart your world piece-by-piece, starting with this bitch and her son, and then your sister. Then, when you can't take anymore, I'm going to cut you limb from limb and leave you in a ditch to die."

"Or…" Jack staggered as he rose to his feet and cracked his neck from side to side. "We can get this over with now, because I'm sick of listening to your bullshit."

Vincent narrowed his eyes. Laying his pistol on the kitchen counter, he pulled two large knives from a rack in the kitchen and tossed one near Jack's feet. Its echo filled the house.

"C'mon, Jack."

"What? You want to give me a fucking cooking lesson?"

Vincent circled the room, tossing his blade from hand to hand as if he was playing a game of tennis and prepping to take his next shot.

"Pick it up," Vincent said.

Jack kept his eyes on him as he reached for it.

"You know, I always wondered why they called you the Butcher. Some say it's because you're good with knives. Others, just brutal. Either way, let's see if you live up to your name."

They stared at each other with death in their eyes.

***

When Dana pried her eyes open, Jason was still clutching her hand. She cast a nervous glance over her shoulder. The sight of Louis' body sprawled out on the ground gave her a moment of relief. Behind him, Frank slumped against a tree, his one hand clasped over his neck, the other barely clinging to his pistol. Dana hurried to him. Dropping to both knees, she pulled back his bloodied hand to inspect the wound. His skin was pale, clammy, and he was going into shock. She was no medic, but with the amount of blood he'd lost, she knew that if he didn't get to a hospital fast, he would die.

"In the car. Call it in," he croaked.

"Don't try to speak."

Tearing off the right sleeve of his shirt, she crumpled it up and pressed it against his neck, then took Jason's hand and had him apply pressure to it while she sprinted to the cruiser. As she passed the house she could hear the sound of a violent struggle; glass shattered followed by several loud thuds, as if someone was breaking the walls of the house.

Inside the cruiser, she snatched up the radio transmitter.

"Officer down. Officer down!" she yelled before giving her location.

***

Back inside the house, it was an all-out war. In a close quarter death match, both of them traded punches in between trying to slash, stab, and end the other's life. Their clothes were torn, showing signs of knife wounds to the legs, arms, and body. From the outside it would have been hard to tell who had the upper hand, since both of them matched each other blow for blow and were equally drenched in blood. The once tidy home now resembled a war zone after a bomb had gone off, as they continued grappling and slamming up against furniture. Shattered glass, split wood, and large chunks of drywall were strewn across the floor. Brawling from room to room, the assault never let up. Each one pummeled the other, inflicting as much pain as they could.

Jack managed to briefly lock his arm around Vincent's throat, trying to choke him out before Vincent drove his head back into his face. Blinking hard, he staggered back, barely registering the pain before feeling the full brunt of a kick striking his ribs. They circled each other, feigning jabs.

As Vincent lunged at him, Jack grabbed his wrist before the knife reached his body, sharply twisting the knife away from himself. In one smooth motion he slammed his fist into his gut, following through by driving his own steely knife up into the pit of Vincent's arm.

Vincent let out a wild, guttural cry, his eyes bulging in agony. Jack tried to parry that with a head butt, but Vincent brought his own knife down into Jack's leg. Searing pain coursed through him, sending him backward. Huffing and panting hard, both men were exhausted. But there was no waiting for the other to recoup before they were back at it.

***

All Dana could see was Jack lying there, motionless. She hadn't seen it happen, but she had heard it. The shattered glass and shards spread all over the gravel told her everything.

"Jack!" she screamed.

Glaring out from where the window once was were the

malevolent features of Vincent. Frantically she turned around for the shotgun that was mounted between the seats, but it was locked. She clutched it, yanking at it with all her strength, but it was no use. There was nowhere to hide; he'd already seen her. As she turned back, it wasn't the sight of him stepping out that frightened her, though that had unnerved her.

It was her son.

He must have heard her cry and sprinted to help. Before she could warn him, Vincent had a firm hold on the back of his collar.

It happened so fast.

"Let him go!" Dana cried, watching Jason flail his arms around before Vincent brought the sharp edge of the knife up to his throat.

"Get over here now!" he bellowed in a gruff voice.

Dana, fearing for her son's life, hurried over.

"Please, don't do this," Dana was crying now.

"Shut the hell up." Dragging Jason by the scruff of his neck, he instructed her to check on Jack. Her eyes darted back and forth between her son and Jack. She shoved Jack, as if trying to wake him from a deep sleep.

"Jack."

***

Jack groaned as his eyelids beat like a bird's wings. Fragments of glass were embedded in his neck. Trails of blood pooled in his clothing. His clothes were torn, and she could see he'd lost a lot of blood from the inside of his thigh.

"C'mon, Jack, don't you die on me yet. I don't want you missing the best part."

Jack heaved, pulling himself up.

"Stay right there." Vincent motioned with his knife at Jason's throat.

Jack could see Vincent's hand trembling; the effect of the wound beneath his arm was draining him of energy. Battered and worn, he cast a glance at the sobbing Dana and then the threat.

"You are getting slow, Jack."

"Let him go, Vincent, and I'll give you a chance to finish me."

Vincent shook his head. A smirk formed. "Women and children. It's an emotional weakness of yours. Does it pain you, Jack, to know that if you had taken care of me years ago when you took my father's life, we wouldn't even be having this conversation? Unlike you, I won't make the same mistake. Now their deaths will be on your hands."

Jack spat a wad of blood out.

"You kill them, you won't get a cent of the money."

Vincent laughed, removing the knife from Jason's throat and tapping it against his own head like a crazed person. "You still don't get it, do you? It's never been about the money."

"So what? You baited me?"

"I adapted. You're not even meant to be alive, Jack. Had things gone right, you shouldn't have walked out of that apartment that day. But you did." He sniffed hard, twirling the knife in his hand as if conducting an orchestra. "Well, shit happens. After you went away, I needed a change of plan. Some way I could kill two birds with one stone. Become a made man, and put a bullet in your head."

"You baited Gafino."

"Now you're catching on. I mean, you and I both know that a quarter of million is nothing compared to what he brings in—but his reputation, now that means everything. I simply dropped a net; he swam into it. When I showed up in this backward town and picked up Matt, he was with his father. Guess he wanted his daddy to bail him out. I told the sheriff he'd get his son back if he cooperated. Which of course was never going to happen, unless he wanted him back in pieces." He chuckled to himself. "Still strikes me as funny what people will say to avoid death. I mean, c'mon, the whole you won't get the money if you kill me is a little overdone, don't you think? But he tried it. Guess he actually did give a shit about his family."

Dana dropped her eyes. Vincent tugged at the back of Jason's collar.

"At least you know your old man tried, kid; that's more than mine did." Vincent directed his attention back to Jack. "Anyway, once you got out, I convinced Gafino to send you to collect the money. I just didn't tell him I was going to kill you before you brought it back. I mean, I couldn't have him killing you now could I?"

"So he knew Matt was dead when he sent me?"

"Of course." He paused. "Oh...you thought these two..." He pointed slowly with the tip of the knife to Dana and Jason. "...were going to change his mind because of your dumbass rule?" He paused to relish the moment. "C'mon, Jack. Hell, I bet you thought you were going to waltz in here, bring back the cash, and walk away." He let out a laugh. "You were dead the second that deal went south. In Gafino's mind, you tainted his reputation, not me. And believe me, Jack. That's all these old timers have left. Their reputation."

For the few times that the knife was not on Jason, Jack was figuring out what to do. His own knife was several feet away. Going for it was out of the question. He didn't stand a chance in hell with his leg wounded.

Thankfully he didn't need to. As Vincent moved the knife away, Jason turned sharply beneath the wounded arm. All Jack could do was watch in horror at the thought of not getting to him in time. In an instant, Jason had twisted free from his grasp.

"Run!" Jack cried.

Propelled away from Vincent, he scrambled, pounding the gravel as he sprinted away.

31

DANA HAD NEVER RUN so far or so fast in her life. Propelled by Jack's words as much as the fear of Vincent harming her son, she put one foot in front of the other and hightailed it around the other side of the house as her son went the other way. Her throat burned and her heart pounded inside her chest.

The last thing she heard before rounding the house was Jack's firm voice. "Vincent, let's finish this."

What she didn't see was that Vincent had taken advantage of Jack's leg wound and took off in pursuit of Jason.

For Dana and Jason, the single thought of escaping was all that mattered now. As they made it to the rear of the house they raced for the dock. Dana caught up with Jason. As she cast a glance over her shoulder, what she saw next made her blood run cold: Vincent.

Vincent's angry voice called out to them. "There's

nowhere to go."

They didn't allow themselves to breathe until they heard the sound of the water. Bursting down the dock, Jason was first in the boat. It was a small fishing boat, white, with a black band around it. Pushing the onboard motor into the water, he began tugging on the cord to start the engine. It coughed and spluttered from years of not being used. Dana was in the process of untying the mooring line when the sound of Vincent's boots hit the wooden dock.

With desperation in his eyes, Jason tried unsuccessfully to get the motor started. Dana didn't stand a chance. Vincent pounced on her faster than a bloodhound.

"Get away from me!" she bellowed.

Tugging her by the back of the hair, he tossed her to the ground. Jason looked on in utter terror.

"Get out of the boat, kid."

He hesitated.

"Now!"

Reluctantly, Jason climbed back up onto the dock. As soon as he was within reaching distance, Vincent took his arm and threw him down by his mother. Dazed and spent from racing to the dock, all Dana could do was grasp her son. With both of them on their knees, Vincent glanced over his shoulder as if making one last check before doing the unthinkable.

"Understand, I find no pleasure in doing this, but he forced my hand," Vincent rasped as he brought up the knife.

Dana wasn't about to let her son die at the hands of some maniacal lunatic. She'd have rather died than let him touch a single hair on her son's head. In full-blown panic mode, she lunged with every ounce of her strength at him.

"Go!" she screamed, putting herself between Jason and Vincent.

Dana struck him in the ribs with a diving tackle that was hard and completely unexpected. Vincent croaked.

In that instant, between life and death, two things had happened. She felt the searing heat of the knife penetrate her shoulder and saw Vincent's knees buckle like a stack of cards. She fell over him, tumbling and rolling. The knife clattered on the dock.

What she didn't know was Vincent had been shot in the leg.

Instinctively her hand reached for her shoulder. When she pulled it back she felt warm, sticky blood. Her heart pumped with adrenaline, her mind blank to the pain. Staring down at the blood, hands trembling, she looked up to see Jack at the far end of the dock. He was dragging one leg but moving forward. In his hands was the sheriff's handgun.

By the time she turned her head to check on Jason, Jack had fired another round, collapsing Vincent's second leg as he tried to get up. Dana didn't hesitate another second to put as much distance as she could between her and Vincent. Jason had already slipped into the water the moment she yelled for him to go. Still swimming in an arc toward the safety of the shore, the sounds of sirens wailing in the distance gave her the smallest amount of relief.

"Go, I'll take care of this," Jack said, his eyes fixed on Vincent.

Gripping her bloodied shoulder, she hurried past him to join Jason.

***

Vincent writhed on the ground in pain, a smear of blood marking where he'd dropped from the first bullet to where he'd dragged himself. The stained wood became a dark shade of crimson.

"I guess you wouldn't consider calling it even?" Vincent said, half-joking as each breath came out as a series of choking gasps.

With little fight left in him, Jack drew close.

"It didn't have to be this way," Jack said as he tried to slow his breathing.

"Of course it did. If not me, someone else would have come."

"Maybe."

"Let me go, Jack. You owe me that."

"I owe you nothing."

As Jack angled the gun, Vincent cried out. "Go on then, shoot me, you coward."

Jack paused with the gun leveled at the man's head. Vincent groaned, letting out his pain through clenched teeth.

"Cowardice is taking the life of a mother and child."

"Then you should know, since you took mine the day you killed my father."

Jack stared into his eyes. Vincent's words cut into him. He was right. All these years he'd lived by a code. A rule that he thought somehow made him different than those in the same line of work. But he was no different. How many mothers and children had been destroyed by the lives he'd taken?

Vincent groaned, gripping his legs.

He shook his head. "Your father would have died either way," Jack said.

Vincent spat at him.

"You think you're better than me?" he asked, steadily crawling his way to the boat. Bloodied fingerprints and a thick smear of blood trailed behind him. The sound of emergency sirens was even louder now. They might have been only minutes away. "We are cut from the same

271

cloth, Jack. Hell, you made me."

Vincent let out a stifled laugh.

"So go ahead, shoot me. Do what you should have done years ago."

"I'm not going to shoot you."

Few would understand what he did next. Jack walked past Vincent, pushing his gun into the small of his back. He took hold of the mooring line and untied it, then walked back with it in his hands. He took hold of Vincent.

"What are you doing?" Vincent croaked.

"Adapting."

With that said, he wrapped it tightly around his neck. All of Vincent's attempts to push him away were futile. His face turned a beet red; his eyes bulged as the rope cut into his neck. Vincent clawed at the rope in utter desperation as Jack returned to the boat. Hopping in, he began emptying the plastic gasoline tank all over the boat. Once done, he tossed it and yanked on the outboard motor's starter cord. One, twice, four more times before it roared to life. Thick coils of smoke rose from it. Leaping back on the dock, he paid no attention to Vincent's strained cries as he frantically attempted to free himself from the coil around his neck. Neither did he watch as his body slipped past him and disappeared beneath the surface of the water.

Only after taking a few more steps did he turn.

For a moment he watched the boat slowly drag Vincent through the water. Within seconds his legs stopped struggling and all that could be heard was the sound of the engine. Jack raised his gun and fired a round at the boat. In an instant, it burst into flames.

He felt no sense of satisfaction after, only pain taking over his body. Knife wounds stung along with what felt like a cracked rib which stole his breath. He'd been operating on pure adrenaline. Now every step back to the shore was excruciating. In the distance, Dana and Jason cautiously approached, but as they did dark walls closed in at the corners of his eyes, squeezing out the light.

Slipping into unconsciousness from the loss of blood, he never felt himself hit the dock.

32

ONCE ROCKLAND POLICE and medics arrived on scene, it felt like she'd been caught up in a sudden sandstorm. Each grain of sand, a question, blasted her mercilessly in the face. Were there more threats? What happened? How many were injured? Who shot who? Her mind whirled, unable to offer them much more than a gesture of the head. Officers were shocked to find Frank clinging to life. Medics began tending to her bleeding. The wound was minor, but felt intensely painful. Dana entered the house to retrieve her purse before leaving, only to find the interior in complete disarray. Blood was splattered and smeared on walls, counters, furniture, and floors. Sitting in the back of an ambulance, she watched as they slid in a stretcher. Jack was still unconscious.

As quickly as they had arrived, they were gone. Out the back of the ambulance window, Dana stared blankly at the wreckage left behind.

***

The emergency room at Rockland Cove's Medical Center was nothing short of chaotic that afternoon. A crowd of patients and families clogged the waiting room and hallways. Nurses in blue scrubs darted back and forth between rooms. With doctors few in number, staff overworked, and an unusual amount of patients, it was lucky if you got seen within six hours. The severest cases were dealt with first, then the rest. This time was no exception. She had only once visited the hospital in all the years she'd lived in the town. Jason had broken his arm falling out of a tree when he was eight. She recalled that the bone had punctured through the skin. Back then she hadn't enjoyed the sight of blood, and this was far worse.

Bloodstained and distraught, Dana burst through the doors behind the paramedics. Jason followed in step. A face full of desperation, her mind hadn't stopped racing even though the bumpy ride in the back of the ambulance had been fast. The moment they were inside, a shock trauma team swarmed them. Respirators covered faces and doctors yelled words like cardiac arrest, he's not breathing, and incubate him.

Dana watched in pure horror as they disappeared through a set of double doors further down the hall.

Her last visual was seeing them wheeled away. Both

looked deathly pale. Frank's body had begun to spasm violently. Jack's remained motionless.

Despite her protests that she was okay, a nurse immediately shuffled her into a separate room as the staff took over. Thankfully her wound required nothing more than a few stitches. Once she had been attended to, she took a seat in the waiting room.

***

As the hands on the clock turned over slowly, the shock of what had taken place began to sink in. There was little to do except reflect. She had trouble holding back tears at the terrifying thought of losing her son and her own life. Wracked by emotional pain that hurt in ways she hadn't experienced before, she braced up under the weight of the event as her mind sifted through the rubble. Faced with the truth of Matt's disappearance, the betrayal of her father-in-law, and Jack's involvement in the whole ordeal, she stared ahead, trying to get a hold on reality.

Trembling, Jason gripped his mother's shaking hand tightly as anxiety coursed through her. Flashing a sideways glance, the corner of her mouth creased ever so slightly, a sign of appreciation or perhaps relief. Still, fear, confusion, and the unknown fought for her attention. Was it really over? Would others come? And what now?

Then her mind would circle back. There was no doubt that if it hadn't been for both of the men, they would be dead. While she was grateful for Frank's change of heart—or need to redeem himself—she couldn't help but wonder about Jack.

He could have fled, she knew that for sure. But he had returned for them at the risk of his own life. Why? It's not like she had given him reason to care in light of his arrest. And what of the money?

She spent the following few hours churning it over even as her friend, Sophie, rushed to her side to offer comfort and aid. An officer briefly took her statement, but wouldn't elaborate on Frank's condition. Between watching people come and go, downing several cups of bitter coffee from a vending machine, and stealing some shuteye on the shoulder of Jason for minutes at a time, she was physically and emotionally exhausted.

She checked in at the nurses' station every thirty minutes like she'd done since arriving. Each time the nurse would tell her there was no new information and reassured her that once they had an update she'd be the first to know. They had suggested she go home, but she felt safer among the crowd of patients. By her eighth trip to the desk, she could hear frustration in the woman's tone. Dana knew better than to pester her any further. She thanked her and returned to the waiting room.

The clock continued to tick over in slow motion. Strangely, Jason appeared to be unfazed by it all, although she knew that couldn't be the case. He was used to burying his worry, only to mention it late at night.

Finally, after what seemed like forever, Jason nudged her. A doctor approached them. She rose to her feet, bracing herself for the worst. She scanned his face for any indication of the outcome, but it gave nothing away.

"I'm Doctor Harris. Would you mind?" He waved his arm, beckoning her toward a set of double doors. After leading her into a quiet area, away from prying eyes and ears, he spoke.

"I was told you are the next of kin for Frank?"

A grim reminder that she was all he had. "That's right, how is he?"

The doctor hesitated before speaking. "I'm afraid he didn't make it."

She clenched her eyes shut, torn by emotion. Despite a part of her that wanted to hate him for turning a blind eye, she couldn't feel anything except pity for him. Frank's single obsession with policing had destroyed his marriage and his relationship with his son. His need to maintain the persona he'd created in the town of Rockland Cove was all he had left. His entire identity was wrapped up in how the townsfolk perceived him. He had known her since she had been a child. After marrying Matt, that bond had only drawn them closer. They had had their differences, and up until Matt's abuse had become evident, they had possessed a mutual respect for one another.

No, it was Matt who should have known better. Everything else was simply the downfall of his actions. She recalled Frank's final words to her as they loaded him into the back of the ambulance at the lighthouse.

"I'm sorry, Dana. For everything."

The memory of those words faded in the doctor's own condolences.

She nodded. "And the other?"

"He's not awake, but he's stable for now."

Her heart lightened ever so slightly. "Do you know when I can see him?"

"You'll have to speak to one of the deputies. We're under strict instructions that no one is to see him."

Dana glanced down the hall. An officer sat in a chair outside a room.

"You should go home. Get some rest. I'll have one of the staff notify you when he's awake."

"Thank you, doctor."

33

T HE LATE AFTERNOON sun hung low over the pines as they returned home. An officer by the name of Flynn Thompson had been given the responsibility of escorting them. Unsure if any other cop was involved, she was a little apprehensive to go with him. But without her vehicle and with him insisting, she had little choice. Previously she'd only met him two or three times when Frank had swung by the house. He was a young cop, fresh out of the academy, who had only just completed his one year probation period. Freshly polished shoes, crisp uniform, and a haircut buzzed tight made him stick out like a sore thumb. He'd always made a point of being polite, unlike some of the other grouchy officers who'd been with the department for far too many years.

On the way back, she inquired if there was a chance she could see Jack, to which he replied in a monotone voice that it wasn't up to him. When asked if he knew why they were preventing anyone from seeing him, he told her that they were investigating the incident and following up on what Frank had told them on the way to the hospital.

She pressed for more details, but he tightened up.

His lips pursed. "Sorry, Dana, I really can't say anymore."

As they approached the motel, Dana noticed that the lot in front had disappeared, only to be replaced by an ocean of faces. Reporters, cameramen, sound engineers, and several locals covered every inch. They passed by seven TV station mobile units along the side of the road, all of which had satellite units on the top and colorful graphic emblems on the sides indicating what station they belonged to. She recognized the local one, but the others were from out of town.

"What the heck?"

"When we get out, just stick close to me," the officer said, flipping his siren on to force the crowd apart.

The mob divided just enough to let the car through. The onslaught of bodies pressed up against the cruiser almost blocked out the light of day as he killed the engine. Like piranhas itching to devour fresh meat, they elbowed each other and shoved their microphones at the windows, vying for that first interview. Dana felt like canned bait.

The very second she cracked the door, a firestorm of

shouting began.

"What's it like to be a survivor?"

"How did you know these men?"

"What is your connection to this New York crime family?"

"Ms. Grant, is this anything to do with your husband's disappearance?"

"Keep back," Officer Thompson bellowed, using his one arm as a barrier and the other to guide her and Jason through the mass.

Dana was at a loss for words. One moment she was about to reply, the next her train of thought was interrupted by another series of questions. Was she meant to answer them? Dana wasn't ready for this. Never in her life had she witnessed such a circus. In the sea of media, her mind spun.

The officer forced his way through the swarm, using as much force as possible. Microphones jabbed against them; Jason swatted them away while doing his best to keep moving forward.

"Get lost."

Nearly trampled by the crowd, the officer pushed back on a cameraman who had managed to knock his hat to the ground. Any attempt at retrieving it was futile. It vanished quickly beneath a centipede number of feet. Soon, questions became incomprehensible. Finally they managed to budge the mass of reporters back enough to climb the steps to the house. Red-faced and panting hard, Dana let out a lungful of air as the door closed behind them. Only the dark silhouette of faces could be seen beyond the glass window.

When Dana entered the kitchen, one glimpse of the damage was enough for her to know that the men must have ransacked the house searching for the money. Officer Thompson followed her into the living room. The sound of his boots on crushed glass made her sigh. Drawers were on the floor, the furniture torn to shreds and photo frames in pieces. She picked up a silver frame containing a photo of them as a family. It reminded her of a time when things had been good. Things weren't always this way, she thought. She sighed again. Turning it upside down, shards of glass fell out. She picked at it, pulling the photo from the frame. The photo showed a much younger Dana with Matt's arm wrapped around her. Jason stood between them, only knee high.

"You don't seem to be able to get a break," Thompson said, sweeping into the next room.

"Nice, they broke the T.V," Jason said, rubbing his hand across the edge of a cracked plasma screen.

After the day they had, the loss of property had zero impact on her. Daily concerns that once seemed insurmountable now paled in comparison.

***

The following few days passed without incident. Satisfied or not, after the police gave their official statement on the events that had transpired the media slowly dispersed. Each morning fewer vans parked outside. Dana watched from behind a curtain as the final remnants slipped away, yesterday's front page news becoming today's fodder. The call to snag a new story soon replaced all and any urge to linger for mere scraps of information on what the police had called a closed case.

Two officers, one of whom was Officer Thompson, were assigned to remain on site until Dana no longer felt threatened or until they themselves were needed. She had taken advantage of their presence by promptly putting them to work on helping her clean up the house. Jason chipped in, and after tossing out most of their damaged possessions, it had left them with very little.

She went about replacing furniture using one of the many thrift stores in town. Where cash flow had been tight before, she knew she was going to max out her credit cards just trying to recoup some sense of normality. Fortunately, though, Sophie, never being one to keep her mouth closed, had rallied together a group of elderly women who ran a collection of boutique stores in the square. She wouldn't tell Dana how she had twisted their arms, but they offered to furnish her place and would not accept no for an answer or any payment. According to them, after learning about her misfortune and her near death experience it was the least they could do.

It was a sweet gesture, and one that she gladly accepted, even though she had doubts about why they were being so charitable. She was quite aware of how things worked in this town. Once this had blown over, she would soon discover the strings. Regardless, for the time being it made her appreciate living in Rockland Cove. Its small town charm and sense of community was hard to find. It extended beyond gossiping old women, antique stores, fishing harbors, and yearly festivals and found its way into their daily lives. It was the one thing that stayed the same, even as the people around her changed.

The funeral for Frank had been arranged for Thursday of that week. A day before, police from all across Maine gathered in the heart of the town to honor his life. Watching behind steel railings under the watchful eyes of locals and members of the department as a stream of cruisers crawled their way through the town, she wrapped her arm around Jason. It was bitterly cold that morning, enough to see her own breath—a stark reminder of how she felt inside. None would know the truth behind Frank's actions, only that he died a hero and gave his life for hers. She chose to show her respect for his final actions by keeping it that way.

Later that evening, she received a phone call from the hospital informing her that Jack was awake, fully expecting to be reminded that she'd have to get police permission to visit. She was surprised to learn that wouldn't be required. The nurse gave her the visiting hour times and was about to hang up when Dana told her to wait.

"So I don't need to speak to a police officer?"

"No, Dana."

"And I can see him tomorrow?"

"Yes, I just said that." The nurse's patience was wearing thin after being made to answer that question three times.

After hanging up, she couldn't help but wonder what had changed. She could have sworn they had told her initially that no one was allowed to see him. Then again, she recalled Officer Thompson mention that Frank had spoken to them on the way to the hospital. She made a mental note to follow up on that.

34

THE NEXT DAY, as she pulled into the hospital around noon, she mulled over questions that she had for Jack. Inside the center it was vastly different to what she remembered. The crowds were gone. The hectic activity had slowed. It was as quiet as any private doctor's office. Order had replaced chaos.

Before going into the recovery room, she took a deep breath. She swung open the door and entered the brightly lit room with the drapes pulled back. An unshaven orderly in white clothing was removing the sheets from the bed. Her eyes shifted to the washroom, which was open and empty.

"Can I help you?"

"Oh…" She scanned the room, looking for any indication of Jack's belongings. "This is room 312?"

"Yes."

"The man in this room, where is he?"

"Gone."

As she turned to leave, assuming that maybe he'd stepped out for a walk, the orderly spoke.

"He asked me to give you this."

"What?" she said, spinning around.

"The gentleman that was in here."

The orderly handed her a piece of folded paper. Confused, her brow knit together. "Tall, dark hair. Goes by the name Jack?"

"Yes, I believe so."

She stared down at the lined paper as the orderly finished up. After tossing the sheets into a blue bag, he tied it off and headed toward the door.

"Excuse me. When did he leave?"

The orderly glanced back.

"Maybe five, ten minutes ago?"

Dana hurried over to the window. She was on the second floor. She scanned below in the car park for him. A family was exiting a minivan, an elderly patient was being wheeled towards the building, and a taxi was stationed outside, but she couldn't see who was getting into it since the awning blocked her view. She watched as the blue and white taxi peeled away, feeling a twinge of disappointment.

Taking a seat on the bed, she unfolded the paper. He'd torn a sheet from a pad on the side table. Scrawled in pencil was a short message. At the top was the Rockland

Cove Medical Center emblem, in blue.

Dana,

I'm not one for long letters, or rambling conversations, so I'll keep this short.

I'm sorry.

I know, it doesn't count for much after all that's happened, but an apology is all I can offer. I wish I could stay longer, but I still have some unfinished business to put behind me.

You are safe. That's all that matters, now.

My whole life it's felt like a dark cloud has been hovering over my head. Every day I live in the regret of my actions. Those I've harmed, those I've let down, and those who I never gave a second chance. At an early age, I bought into a lie, one that has cost more than I can fathom. I'm not looking for sympathy in telling you this, only that you might know why I returned to you and Jason.

After my stint in Rikers, all I wanted was to forget the past and leave behind the terrible things I'd done—and start anew.

Then all this happened. Caught between a rock and hard place, I made another wrong decision. I honestly didn't see it playing out like this. But regardless, being here, with you, I saw a glimmer of what that new life might have looked like beyond the past, away from the city, in Rockland Cove.

Dana, I know I've made wrong choices, told a thousand

lies, endangered those close to me and committed acts of violence that no one should expect to go unpunished. Hell, any penalty less than death would be undeserving for what I am guilty of in this life.

After getting out, I guess I had hoped to escape that.

I know now how naïve I was.

How foolish to think I could walk away unscathed.

If anything, my previous line of work has shown me that no one can ever outrun his or her past. Or truly hide from who they've become.

We are the sum total of all our experiences, for good or bad.

Eventually, all our sins catch up and demand payment.

Of that I'm certain.

Now maybe there is a higher power behind this life that governs our steps, maybe not. Perhaps we are all just dealt a hand and have to play what we hold and accept the outcome.

But is that it? Is it too late to try and change who we are?

For the longest time I thought it was.

You see, when you've spent your entire life lost at sea with only one trajectory—a collision course with jagged rocks— you don't expect to survive. You're fully aware that as you bear down on the immovable, it will smash you to pieces.

You accept this. You resign to one's fate.

In many ways, if I'm honest, I've been shipwrecked for a long time.

Until you. Like a speck of light in the darkness.

Offering a faint glimmer of hope.

A shimmering distraction that beckoned me.

With you, I felt I had a reason to turn the wheel.

Like a lighthouse keeper.

You didn't strike me as someone concerned about what kind of crew was at the helm of the ship or where it had sailed, or what cargo it carried.

Instead, you offered more than a glimmer of hope. You allowed me to see a way out of the endless storm. A clear path to the safety of a shoreline.

Deserving rescue or not, a lighthouse keeper treats everyone with the same courtesy.

I'm indebted to you, for that.

Well, I guess I rambled a little more than I should have, so let me wrap this up. I've left you something. You'll find it inside the heavy bag in the basement. I'm sure you will know what to do with it.

Trust me when I say that no one will come looking for it.

Yours,

Jack

As warm sunshine bathed Dana's face, she took a moment to collect her thoughts before rising. She slowly closed the paper and pocketed it.

Returning home that afternoon, she ran a few errands

in town and then collected Jason from school. Waiting outside, she could feel the other moms' eyes on her. If they had an accusing eye when Matt went missing, what did they make of her now?

Both Dana and Jason were quiet inside the truck on the short journey back. The past week had taken its toll on them. A solemn cloud had overtaken Rockland Cove. The town had lost more than a sheriff that day; it had lost its innocence to acts of violence unheard of in years prior. The emotional upheaval was to be expected. Each of them dealt with it in their own way. Jason would head off to his room. Some folks turned to the bottle after traumatic events. She would retreat to the yard; Dana turned to nature. Getting her hands in fresh soil, pulling weeds, and planting was therapeutic.

On the final stretch, she flipped down the truck's visor to block the blinding light. Between the white and gray clouds that drifted steadily on the horizon, the afternoon sun made her eyes ache and did little to alleviate her throbbing head. Mentally exhausted, her mind flashed unbidden to the letter.

***

Jason was the first inside, retreating almost instinctively to his bedroom. She heard his door shut. She hadn't mentioned the letter to him, only that Jack had been discharged from hospital and wasn't one for goodbyes. She could tell that it bothered her son. They had bonded, of that she was certain. Sure, he had taught him a thing or two that she wasn't keen on. But he'd come out of his shell, gained confidence, and opened up to her when Jack was around. That much she could see.

Curious, she headed for the basement. Pulling the cord hanging beside the door, she switched the light on and descended down the wooden steps. She hadn't kept much down there, besides Jason's drums, boxes, and some oversized black bags. It was unfinished, and had stayed that way ever since they'd taken possession of the property.

It's inside the heavy bag. She recalled what he had said.

This could take a while, she thought, looking at the numerous black bags and several plastic storage containers she'd need to shift to get at them.

"Jason!" she shouted up.

No answer.

"Can you give me a hand?" she bellowed beneath the open vent. A tin voice echoed back.

"Be right down."

She had shifted a container full of photo albums by the time he joined her.

"What are you looking for?"

"Just give me a hand; I need to get at these bags."

"There's nothing in those except winter clothes, boots,

and your old teacher books."

She tossed him a look.

He hesitated a second. "I should know. You made me spend an entire Saturday sorting through it all."

"Well, which one looks the heaviest?"

"What?"

"Jack said it's in a heavy bag."

Jason frowned.

"He left us something. He said it was in a bag, a heavy one."

Jason dropped a bag he was holding, and moved over to the black punch bag that hung from the rafters. Silver letters that spelled out the word EVERLAST ran horizontal across the top. Tightly coiled around the mid-section were strips of grey masking tape. Most gyms used it. It was a common way to hold in the filler and seal up cracked leather. No one would have batted an eye, but Jason picked at a corner of tape that was already partly lifted. Dana stared on. Tearing it back, he began unwrapping it.

Then she saw it.

Instead of it containing nothing more than sand, shredded fabric, or foam, wads of green hundred dollar bills spilled out along with shredded fabric like an overweight belly being unleashed from a strong belt. Each packet was less than half an inch thick.

As more cash fell out of the gash in the side of the punching bag, the wider Dana's jaw dropped open.

35

When Jack entered The Pigs Ear late that evening, he knew there was a good chance he wouldn't walk out again. Only four of Gafino's men were in the gym. Two fighters in the ring stopped sparring momentarily to gawk, as if witnessing a skid row inmate making the final journey to be executed.

By all accounts, he should have been dead.

The fact that he had survived was surprising, but that he had the nerve to return must have looked like pure madness. With his face steadfast and the leather duffel bag full of money in hand, he climbed the steel steps that led to Gafino's office. His boots beat out a steady rhythm.

Behind the glass door, Gafino was waiting for him seated behind a desk. Drinking a glass of brandy, he studied Jack. His eyes dropped to the bag.

"Always on time."

Jack dropped the bag in front of him with a thud.

"That's it. It's over."

Gafino unzipped it and glanced briefly inside.

"It's all there."

"And Vincent?"

Gafino's eyes flicked up to his. Jack's lack of response said it all. He chuckled to himself.

"Can't trust anyone these days." Unflinching, Jack stood firm. Gafino downed another gulp of the amber-colored liquor. "But you. I could always rely on you to tell me the truth. You weren't complicated like the others. You and me, we have an understanding. For better or worse, we know what needs to happen to get things done. That's rare, Jack. There are those who live by rules, and those who make them. We make them."

"I only have one."

"That's right. And you've never broken it, have you, Jack?"

Jack studied him. "So we're good?"

"If you've tied up all loose ends, yeah."

Their eyes locked. "Yeah."

Gafino smiled, a glint in his eyes. He inhaled deeply and downed the remainder of his brandy.

Jack nodded and turned to leave.

"You sure you want to do this?" Gafino asked.

When he reached the door, Jack cast a glance back.

"By the way, Jack, I was thinking of stopping by and visiting your sister. You know, for old time's sake."

Jack didn't pause, since he knew what that meant.

"You sure you don't want to rethink your decision?"

"See ya', Roy."

As the door closed behind him, he didn't look back. Any other man would have expected a bullet in the back of the head. Jack didn't. He knew Gafino too well. That wasn't his way. It was too fast, too easy, and not painful enough. He got off on seeing the agony in the eyes of his victims. It was never about the money. In many ways, Gafino was right about how alike they were; in others, not so.

Outside the air was like a cool balm against his skin. Jack strolled toward his Impala. Then, from behind him, an enormous explosion erupted. The Pig's Ear disappeared in a cloud of dark smoke and an inferno of flames. Fireballs of debris fell like rain. Unflinching, Jack didn't look back or give a second thought to whether the blocks of C4 placed beneath the top layer of money inside the bag had killed Gafino.

No one was walking away from that alive.

A moment later, he slipped behind the wheel of his car, threw the remote detonator onto the passenger seat, and turned over the ignition. The reflection of flames dancing on his rear window faded as the Impala peeled away into the distance.

36

DOWN AT ROCKLAND COVE MARINA, Jack's boat was moored alongside a vast line of schooners that bobbed in pristine waters. It was a classic, natural, wooden lobster boat that now doubled as his home and livelihood. A deep New England red with a white interior made it blend in. Nothing flashy. Nothing that would attract unwanted attention. It had become his new way of life. Unlike the magnificently rigged fifty-five foot schooners that towered over his and provided tourists with two hour sailing trips around the bay, his paled in comparison. But it belonged to him and was simple, much like the life he'd longed to lead. Whether it was beneath the stars at night or the glaring heat of the sun, he'd never felt as unshackled and free as he had in those days. For four days a week he offered local tourists scenic coastal excursions, and on occasion he would show them how lobster was caught, just as the previous owner had taught him.

Almost two months had passed since that fateful night at The Pig's Ear. It was the final nail in a coffin for a life that was now dead to him. One final act of violence that marred his soul but gave him a second chance. Ridding himself of Gafino was the only way he could save his sister, clean his slate, and walk away. Few escaped life in the mob; even fewer on their own terms. Most either died or fled into hiding behind a new identity in an unknown location to live the life of a snitch. Forever glancing over their shoulder, forever living on borrowed time. One thing they all knew was that eventually everyone wound up dead, either from the hands of another or by suicide. Life inside organized crime didn't make sense to anyone who'd never been in it. But to those who grew up in it, it was all they had ever known.

The familiar held a strange comfort, even if it was destructive. It was a brotherhood, a culture, and lifestyle that would continue to attract the ignorant. In hindsight it all seemed clear; it was nothing more than a young man's game of ego, greed, and stupidity. No, unlike those who hid and spent each night in fear of retribution, Jack slept like a baby in those months, whether he'd made peace with his demons or simply let go of the need to be in control. The past was just that: the past. Its only reach on him was in nightmares, and even those had become less. He never gave another thought to it.

Then there was Dana. He didn't regret his life before her. It had led him to her. Whether that was for the right or wrong reasons, whether she would give him a second chance…

It didn't matter now.

In the early afternoon, Jack returned from The Shack on the Marina. Part restaurant and part store, it offered some of the best lobster in the area along with steep discounts to those who made their living on the water. Maine's yearly lobster festival had put it on the map. Its fame had spread throughout the town and well beyond. Residents from three counties over would travel just to taste its unique selection on the menu. If they could stick lobster in it, it was for sale. Fried, boiled, grilled, baked—they offered the works. Since returning, he rarely ventured beyond the Marina. All the basics he needed were there. Fishing tackle, amenities, and, most importantly, obscurity.

Jack strolled around the winding dock. The planks creaked beneath his boots. The water sloshed and lapped up against the boats. The sky was a quilt of colors as a gentle breeze blew in. It wouldn't be long before the summer would be over and boats would be hauled into storage.

Jack cupped a hand over his eyes to shield them, trying to make out the person standing close to his boat. When it became clear, his pace slowed.

"Dana?"

She turned. "Hi, Jack."

"I hardly recognized you."

She motioned to her hair, which had changed.

"You look well."

"You too." She paused, pushing a hand into her back pocket and shifting from one foot to the other.

"So when were you going to tell me you were back in town?"

Dropping the remainder of his coffee into a bin, he stepped a little closer. "Besides the obvious? I didn't exactly think I was someone you would want to see again."

Her eyes fixed on his; she nodded, as if weighing his answer.

"Jason asks about you."

"How's he doing?"

"You know." She cocked her head to one side. "The usual teenage angst. He has a girlfriend now, so I see him even less. A nice girl, though."

Jack nodded, taking a moment to take her in. She wore tight jeans, the knees worn. Flip flops, and a thin white summer top. She'd changed her hair. Gone were the long flowing locks; in its place was a short bob that suited her. A rush of memory from their time together came back in a series of images. Her body tangled up in his; her hot mouth over his.

"Nice boat. I hear you're doing tours?"

He nodded. "Yeah…Doesn't exactly pay well, but I don't need much."

They stood for a moment studying each other before he looked away.

"I sold the motel."

"How about that. That's good."

"Yeah, it's nice to not have that on my plate. I'm at the lighthouse, and helping Sophie out at her store part-time."

"Ah, yeah, she was quite the character."

"Still is. Yeah, I used the money that…" She trailed off before continuing. "About that, eh…"

He rested his hand against the boat. "No need to say anything."

She pursed her lips. "Right, well, I just wanted to thank you."

He wasn't too sure how to reply to that. It wasn't as if it was his money. Instead he simply nodded.

It was a strange feeling that came over him; he wondered if it was mutual. Seeing her again wasn't like visiting an old friend; it was different. Not quite strangers, and yet as if they were meeting for the first time. Under different circumstances, the way it should have been.

Even though only two months had passed, he wasn't quite sure why he felt uncomfortable, whether it was his role in the whole event that had transpired or the fact that a day hadn't gone by without him thinking about her.

"Well, maybe I'll see you around?" she said.

"Yeah. Maybe."

"It's good to see you, Jack."

"You too."

She looked as if she had more to say, but chose to hold it in. She gave a slight smile, then put out her hand.

Awkwardly he went to shake it, and it went from a shake to a hug. Both of them appeared to recognize the awkward nature of the situation, and neither of them knew how to respond.

Parting, Dana flashed one last smile and then turned.

Jack watched her make her way up the dock. He wrestled with his thoughts. A part of him wanted to turn and leave it all behind, but somewhere deep inside he just couldn't.

"Do you want to get a beer?" he shouted.

She glanced back, and bit down on the side of her lip. "Sure." Making her way back to him, she continued. "You know we can't pick up where we left off, right?"

"Yeah, I realize that."

"Things have changed."

"I get it."

She stopped in front of him. "But we can start afresh."

"That's all I've ever wanted."

She cocked her head to one side and extended her hand to him.

"Dana Grant."

He smiled, shaking her hand.

"Jack Winchester."

* * *

THANK YOU FOR READING

The Debt Collector

Debt Collector 2: Vengeance is Available

Please take a second to leave a review, it's really appreciated. Thanks kindly, Jon.

IF YOU ENJOYED THIS BOOK...

Please take a moment to leave a review, even if it's only a few lines. It really is appreciated more than you could imagine. I always like to know what my readers thought. Most importantly, it helps other potential readers decide if they should give it a shot. Without reviews an author's book is practically invisible online.

ABOUT THE AUTHOR

Jon Mills is originally from England. He now lives in Ontario, Canada. Jon Mills is the author of the thrilling teen trilogy Undisclosed, The Promise, The Debt Collector Series, Lost Girls, I'm Still Here, and many books under various pen names. He can be reached through his website at www.jonmills.com. You can also connect with him through Facebook at www.facebook.com/authorjonmills or on Twitter at www.twitter.com/Jon_Mills. You can send all email to contact@jonmills.com

Made in the USA
Middletown, DE
05 September 2021